Barracuda

Bytch

"I got niggas on speed dial…"

Karla Denise Baker

Library of Congress Control Number: 2009935954
ISBN-13: 978-0-9815668-6-3
ISBN-10: 0-9815668-6-3

Printed in the United States of America
10 9 8 7 6 5 4 3 2 1

Barracuda Bytch - first paperback

photographer: Don Sherrill

Email: karlabkr@yahoo.com
www.facebook.com/karla.d.baker
Formatting/editing: Karla Denise Baker
Model: Karla Denise Baker

THE WRITE MESSAGE

The Write Message P.O. Box 3071 Paterson, New Jersey 07509

Other books by Karla Denise Baker:

Anonymous

Spittin' 'Em Out Like BABIES

Sleepin' Wit' the Virus (a sequel to Anonymous)

Does God Have Toys in Heaven? (a memoir)

To all you bullshit muthafuckers, I hope when you read this book you take heed to when a woman is fed da fuck up!!!! Oh, oh, you bitches need to take heed too. No…your asses aren't off the hook because sometimes its your damn fault a *clean* muthafucker turns *dirty*.

In the words of Mae West,
(August 17, 1893- November 22, 1980)

"A hard man is good to find."

(In the words of Chocolate Twat),

"Ain't that the muthafuckin' truth."

"A woman is like a $1.00 bill.
A $1.00 bill goes from hand-to-hand,
A woman goes to man-to-man."
—Anonymous

U Dirty Whore

if I had to recount on each toe
each time a man's words cut
the vocal cord of my sound
i'd probably asphyxiate
gurgling from my saliva
my womanhood shedding like sheep skin
of my mahogany-light
i might scratch the surface of my cortex
the pupil of my sight may blur
menstruating out my frustrations
bleeding tears of anguish
as if a child abandon by unfilled fatherly shoes.

if I had to recount on each hand
the times I'd cry Blige blues and Badu
asking her why Tyrone can't
calm the motions of my nerves
that shake uncontrollably
hearing the growling of my weariness
in the essence of my womanhood
i'd bellow like screams of a homeless man
being stabbed
stretched out on the dark pavement of death
and ask humbly
why do I keep eyeballing the same circumstance
the same shhhhhhhiiiitttttttt!!!!!
soaking in Dizzy Gillespie's Epsom salt
fiend like a junky offa dope
beating that bitch
over, and over, and over again
fucking me till no tireless end
blind by the agony of blood shedding
from my pussy
dripping and drenching
the lining of my boy shorts
in a pool of murkiness
lathering like soap in a daze of hopelessness
i lay fetal

BARRACUDA BYTCH- Karla Denise Baker

shattered like busted bottles
smashed like beer cans for a refund of a nickel
my brain is tipsy and motions slow mobility
witnessing an execution of my mind
lingering stench of sweaty coochie
awakens my nostrils
sniffing in dirty raw dick
defecating a bad dream of what da hell
there are no signs to rescue my abduction
i am too frail to defeat the evil of the streets
too stress to straighten the kinks of nappy
or verbalize the unhappiness
that blisters my soles
in the vessels of my subconsciousness
i lay reminiscing of that girl who lay bludgeoned
decaying the taste of penis residue upon my tongue
smearing pussy cream upon my lips
glossin' the chap away
polishing the clearness of my toenails black
shadowing my eyelids fire engine red
lingering a fragrance of whorish
as dogs bark
predators scratch their balls
i flinch by the inevitable
that slaps and smacks me upon my dirty ass
painting my body in watercolors
if only someone hadn't snatched
my coat that wintry day
my nakedness would've never been exposed
trembling as i stagger while powdering my nose
wandering obliviously
feelin' the ache in my soul
that wails in a newborn cry
mudslinging consciousness in six inch stilettos
pausing to sit
legs rise mid-air
lettin' that coochie breathe a bit
till the next comes
wanting me to travel down south
pubic hairs stuck in between my thoughts
DNA of his reality
purging come to disremember.

if I had to recount each time
i'd probably still exist
in the memory of his, his, his, his, his mind
hearing my laughter sing
sniffing the fragrance of delusional love
nicotine of cancer
residue of his ejaculation
that sickened my cervix
coughing up blood
phlegm breaking me up inside
slowly gutting out the twinge that devoured my essence.

if I had to recount
i'd flashback to the day, time, month, and year
i'd quench the thirst of my genetics
a whoremonger and his trick
dad ate mommy's pussy
and mom sucked daddy's dick.

if I had to recount
there is no question that i am a blessing in disguise
how many live to tell their story
how many die
???????

Barracuda
Bytch

BB Talk

For all you busted bitches, I'm gonna school y'all on how you can reinvent yourself. Do a come back like Whitney Houston. Listen; if you have *never* experienced a sexual orgasm I might turn you out to be a sexual fiend. I am not liable for your actions so don't go blaming me if you get a Big One that you can't handle. I warned you ahead of time. If you are still wiping your ass with baby wipes this is not for you. Consider yourself warned!!!!!!

Just like anything else in life you have to want it. You have to eat, sleep, and shit it out! You have to work those muscles. Feel the pain. Get your weak ass up and do it all over again, and again, and again. That's right! You have to look yourself in the mirror and get pissed off by who looks back at you. That busted bitch! You have to put yourself on a regimen: food, water, and dick. Use your "gift" (pussy) to your advantage, dammit! You have to work the *pussy*. Work it! Work da hell out of it! Groom that kitty up! Comb her nappy head. Spray some Afro sheen on her ass. Then and only *then*, do *you* get your fuck on! Just make sure you got your female condom in check. We don't want any mishaps.

Listen bitches, I know how to work *my* twat. I did not stutter. I said *twat*. Who am I? I am every forty-year-olds worst enemy. Thirty year olds despise me because I make 'em look bad. Twenty year olds are giving me my due respect. And these skanky bitches out here who think some stank pussy is going to keep their baby boys happy know not to fuck wit' me 'cos I'll play those amateur 'hood rats out. I'll have these skanky bitches giving *head* for a nickel and tell 'em to keep a penny for change 'cos that's how much their dirty pussies are worth. A goddamn penny! That's right! No, you don't want to fuck wit' me because I will rain all over your parade and snatch your man right from under your nose. But don't fret ladies…finders is not keepers.

Who am I? I am that big and beautiful chick from DeWitt, New Jersey. Remember chunky 200-pound chick. Yeah, I bet you don't. Well, as you can see I am not big and chunky anymore. I am sexy, sultry, and seasoned succulence.

Twats…listen here, huh. I am a sixty-something year old seasoned twat who can't get enough of a tight fist doing me strong. I love a man who likes a dominating woman. Sure you can swagger your dick like you da man on the outside. Do you, Boo! But best believe inside I got control. Who am I? My name is Chocolate Twat. Maybe you've heard of me. Maybe you haven't. But after reading this book everyone will know who da fuck I am.

Kake Mahogany, I heard about *you*. Sister-girl, I got yo back. Done Deal isn't he *your* man. Oops, my bad (smirking). Well, between him and Dick String-A-Long, they're just my playmates. Ladies, there are certain qualities I look for in *your* men. A *lady* never tells. Let's just say you all got comfortable and *I* got wit' it.

As a little girl my aunt Priscilla always told me to never leave home without an extra umbrella just in case I lost one. Aunt Priscilla was on the prowl for another umbrella (dick). Well, on the real I feel like I'm losing my husband Whupp so I have my extra umbrella on the side—dripping wet.

Listen, this young, vivacious woman is about to school y'all. When someone is trying to step in my domain I don't play games. I will break out the karate and hurt somebody. Don't you know that I am a black belt? I will black da fuck out on your ass! Look, I know that I am a handful—a piece of fuckin' work. Yes, yours truly is not only mouth I know how to use it well. And with this body, this twat, and my natural beauty I will make your head spin. I ain't nobodies joke, but in the end I always *cum* out on top.

On the real though, I have been a bucket of cum since my mama showed me how to insert one of 'em tampons up my twat. I was wide open after that. Anytime my period would come I would be thrilled, you hear me. Thrilled! Why? 'Cos that gave me a legitimate reason to gently arouse myself as I was inserting that stick of cotton up inside me. It was just the right size to make me tremble. I loved getting my period. But I hated what came with it. Those damn cramps. Every woman should know what I am talking about. Then the bloating got in my way. The worst was when my nipples would be tender to the touch. *Ouch!* My body was screaming for some Midol. After a while I hated getting my period, but I loved the sensation of something being inserted inside of me. I knew once I got the real thing I was going to be a handful. And sure 'nough I was. I was too much for my man to hold and handle.

I am one of 'em women who adore herself. Call me vain I really don't give a fuck. I love everything about myself: looks, silk-like hair, titties, waistline, hips, ass, and the illustrious pussy. Now how many women can say that they love *everything* about themselves? I bet you not many. I'd put my mouth on that but you might like it. Lol.

Prologue

"*Oooooooooooooooooooh ba-bbbbbbby*, get it, baby! Do it, baby. C'mon, baby, get it, get it...*ooooooooooooh, baby*, I feel it cumming...*oh, shit, oooh, oooh, oooh*!!!..." I seductively moan and groan while standing on top of my head with my legs in a V position, breathing erratically.

Done is standing on top of my mahogany leather chair with his hairy legs spread standing on the balls of his feet fucking me from behind. His massive hands grip both of my legs to get a better feel and thrust harder.

My eyes flicker as my arms are getting tired, but I am hanging in there like a trouper. "Oh baby, that feels good. Talk to me, *baby*. Talk dirty to me." I moan, and then wet my lips with saliva.

Ring, ring, ringgggggggggggggggggggggggggggg...

"Don't stop! Keep goin'...keeeppppp goin'...shhhitttt!" I slur while squinting my eyes as he is diggin' so sweetly in *my* pussy.

"Don't answer it, baby. Oh shiiiittttttttttt, ooooh, I'm cumming! I'm *cummin'*...Damn, baby!"

"*Fuck, Fuck, Fuck.*" Done murmurs as he shoots cum all over my ass.

My mouth widens like that porn star Kapri Styles in *Addicted to Black Crack 1*. I damn near scream out *his* name but I mute myself by tightening my lips. All I feel is slimy wetness around the lips of my pussy. Done gets off the chair and helps me down like a true gentleman. My legs feel wobbly as I stand before him with disheveled hair and pussy juice streaming down my legs onto my expensive ass carpet. At this moment I don't give a fuck. I lean in

12

and lick his left nipple and inch my hand down to his weak cock and squeeze it for a job well done. I smirk 'cause I killed the worm.

Before I get a chance to have Done lick Lil' Baa-Baa (my hot pussy) the damn phone rings.

Ring, ring, rinnnnnnnnnnnnnnnnnnngggggggg...

Finally I answer the phone. "Hello." I say in a pretend sleepy voice.

"Oh, I apologize, um, did I wake you, Mrs. Twat?"

"Well, I had dozed off for a minute or two. Who's calling?" I say as I sit on the edge of my Simmons Beautyrest mattress while Done stretches his naked body across my bed and shuts his eyes.

Shit! This muthafucker is going to sleep.

"Sorry about that. Um, my name is Song Byrd. I'm a journalist and the publisher and sole owner of *What Ticks* magazine. I don't know if you've ever heard of it. Anyway, I don't know if you remember but I called you last week in regards to hearing your speech at the *Violence Against Women Act* fundraiser held at the Brownstone in Paterson, New Jersey. You talked about what occurred with Vernetta Cockerham—the African-American woman from North Carolina. She used to reside in Paterson years ago. She used to work in the records room of the Paterson Police Department."

"Hmmm?" I have to take a minute to reboot my memory bank. "Oh, yes, the name rings a bell. I read that article in the August (2009) issue of *O* magazine. Tragic. Her (second) *husband* used to torment her. He threatened to kill her. I can't believe he did that to her baby—killed her seventeen-year-old daughter Candice. That really made my blood boil."

"I know that this is short notice but I was wondering if we could meet for a few hours, today, if possible. I apologize for the inconvenience."

"Song Byrd, you say your name is? Why do you want to interview me? I've never experienced domestic violence." I cut my eyes to the side staring at the photo of me when I was a chunky little girl.

Silence.

"You seemed very opinionated about the subject. That's what piqued my interest. You weren't afraid to speak up—to make noise—to roar with outrage. If you've never experienced you sure made it seem like you had. I mean the emotion in your voice spoke loudly in my ears. It sounded like an outcry."

"No, I'm just talkative. My dad always taught me to never be afraid to speak up. Well, I guess the subject hit a nerve. But if you feel that I can be of some sort of assistance I'll be happy to meet with you. This might turn into my life story." I chuckle. "'Cos I got a lot to say."

"That would be exciting! Say around noon."

"Sure. Noon. My address is 277 Liverpool Way. It's the yellow house on the right. See you then. Good-bye."

As I hang up the phone I turn and look at Done, "Listen, you gotta go before Whupp wakes up. I dunno how long he is going to hibernate in the basement. Let me make sure the coast is clear before you head out, okay."

Done cut his eyes at me with a grimace on his face. "Why don't you leave that sorry cat, huh?"

He is really getting on my last nerve. "I can't. He's my husband!" I snap.

Done sort of twists his lips and droops his eyes showing a hint of jealousy. "Yeah, aiight. I can't tell 'cause I'm the one hittin' it."

I smirk. "That you do, baby, so stay in your *position* and we'll be alright. We don't have time to be catching feelings and shit. We just kickin' it, right?" I wait for him to respond.

"Yeah, Twat. We just kickin' it."

"Well, stop buggin'. You know this good pussy ain't going nowhere. Listen, I'll call you when I want the dick, okay."

"Yeah, baby…yeah."

"Now get your fine ass out of here before our covers are blown."

I open the bedroom door and walk into the hallway to make sure the coast is clear. I wave my head for him to c'mon. We ease down the stairs and I quietly open the front door and send him on his way. As I am about to close the door I hear Whupp say, "Honey, you going somewhere in your nightclothes?"

I keep it cool. Then I kneel down and grab his morning paper. "No, baby, I thought I heard the paperboy. Would you like your paper waiting for you on the kitchen table? How about your favorite wheat pancakes toppled with fresh strawberries for breakfast?" I ask, as I turn to sashay in the kitchen with a sly grin on my face.

"Sure, honey." I hear him say, none the wiser.

***

The doorbell rings at exactly noon. I rush to answer the door in my wife beater T, Capri's, and Coach flip-flops. As soon as I open the door there is this brightness on the face of this petite white woman with a Mohawk of bright red hair and an ass as big as mine. *Someone's been sticking her good*, I think to myself. She speaks with a London accent as she introduces herself.

"Hello. Mrs. Twat, I'm Song Byrd. This is my cameraman Snow." Snow is tall, dark-skinned with dark eyes, and a muscular physique dressed in a white dress shirt and fitted Lucky Brand jeans. He is eye candy, I must say. Eye-Candy!

"Come in." I say, as I can't help but to take a glimpse of Snow's ass. *Yum.*

I give them the grand tour of four bedrooms, three bathrooms, two full kitchens of steel appliances, new hardwood floors, and fireplace on the patio deck.

I turn and say. "The two door garage leads to our fully furnished basement. That's where my hubby likes to hide." We continue to view the house.

"Is your husband here?" Song asks as she stops on the top step, crisscrosses her pale arms about Ed Hardy T-shirt and crisscrosses her legs at the ankles as her bootleg jeans cover her black leather Aldo boots that makes her look slightly taller than 5'1". Her right hand caresses the mahogany banister as she feels its smooth and rich refinement. From there we proceed to walk downstairs as I escort them into the dining room.

"No. He's not one to like the spotlight. He ran out for a few hours to let me do this interview." I say with sort of a smirk on my face.

"Oh. Well, this is a lovely, lovely home, Mrs. Twat." Song says with her ice-blue eyes sparkling like crystal.

I say, "Thank you. There's much more to see, but we can do that later. If you'd like we can setup in the living room. Would you like some tea, coffee, or spring water?"

"Water, would be fine." says Song.

We walk into the luxurious living room smothered in ancestral history, collectibles, and shelves of African-American literature, architecture, fashion, self-help, and many, many other books to stimulate the mind. "How about you, sir, would you like anything to drink?"

Snow speaks with a sexy country accent that tingles my lips down below. I stand undressing him with my eyes. I bet he is awesome in bed. Those countrymen really know how to put it on a sister. At least that's what I've heard from one of my old acquaintance that used to date a man from Charlotte, North Carolina. She said he putta hurtin' on her coochie. Liked to put her out of work for nearly a month, so she said. Said his cock was so powerful that she became addicted needing to have it at least every fours hours or so. I thought she was full of shit, but I can't say she didn't leave me curious. Hmmm? I sure wonder if there's any truth to her tale. I sure wonder.

As I resume back to reality I find myself smirking as I hear Snow say. "Nothing for me, ma'am."

I kinda smile with my eyes. "You sure? It's no imposition."

He looks at me with a smile on his handsome face. "I'm sure, ma'am."

"Oooooo-kay. Well, make yourselves comfortable while I get some refreshments."

As I walk out of the living room I put a little sway in my hips hoping Snow is sneaking a quick peek of my derriere, but I don't turn around to see. I think he did, though, because I have a nice ass.

I return back into the living room with a tray of beverages and finger sandwiches. Song is sitting comfortably on the chocolate three-piece sectional with stone-colored micro-fiber seat cushions as Snow sits on the matching swivel chair as he rests his camera on the cocktail ottoman. Then he stands to position his camera on his broad left shoulder.

"Here you go." I hand Song a bottle of Poland spring water. I sit right beside her on the couch and adjust my *girls*. Snow happens to catch a glimpse and smirks.

"I just want to say thanks for doing this, Mrs. Twat. We'll just talk like girlfriends do. You know girlfriends who haven't seen each other in years. Feel free to express yourself, okay."

"Gotcha."

Song turns towards her cameraman. "Okay, Snow, we're ready."

This is my debut. Lights. Camera. Action.

TWAT

Today I woke up in the wee hours with a *hard-on*. Yeah, I had a hard-on in my mind so it was critical that I did something about it. I mean it was *hard*. Girllllll, I could see it vividly as if it was standing at attention waiting for me to climb on top and ride it like a cowgirl. Now the good thing about this hard-on was that I knew the owner. Yep. If it were ever reported missing I'd be the one to give a positive description: long, thick, light-skinned with a bulging head and a little pee-pee hole with two teeth marks just around the tip of the head. I just so happened to be a little tipsy off of a shot glass of Barracuda Bytch I had earlier in the day. That's right! I invented my own concoction. Well, as you can imagine my drink is potent so I accidentally grazed my teeth and broke the skin on his dick. I know my own teeth marks, okay. Well, now he is walking around with teeth tattoo on his dick. 'Ey shit happens.

The one thing I thought to do was to get dress and drive over to *his* house. Use my key. Climb into bed with him (*while his wife was asleep laying next to him*) and get my fuck on. But that would've been a little crazy. Don't get it twisted I'ma crazy bitch, but not that crazy. So I did the alternative. I pleasured myself until my eyes nearly crossed in the back of my head, toes curled until they cramped up on me, and my middle finger nearly got jammed from vigorously stroking my clit until I almost had a goddamn seizure. Shit, I came so hard that I thought I was having a heart attack or a stroke. I went through all of that trouble just to get a nut. But it was worth it.

Don't get me wrong I was hungry for that *young dick*, but see I knew that I had options. I got niggas on speed dial. I never had to worry about *dick*. Don't be silly. Honey, those days were over for me. But if I think back to the way it used to be. Chile, I'd probably be a nun. Thank god, Sexy Pain (my aunt Erby whom I might add is serving time in prison for killing her boyfriend) came knocking on my bedroom door and gave me a pep talk about the coochie when I was justa kid. Of course, none of her womanly advice made any sense to me as a child or teen, but by the time I met womanhood it made all the sense in the world. Aunt doesn't know it but she created a nymphomaniac.

***

DeWitt, New Jersey

"Lawd, Chocolate, is bigger than Sherrie and the chile is only two!" aunt Erby with her lazy-eye and halitosis breath smellin' like an alcohol factory always loved to instigate some gossip. And lemme tells y'all once she got started there was no stoppin' her until her young buck called blowin' up her cell phone. While aunt Erby was sweet talkin' to her boo my big breasted aunt Gird who was blacker than tar, but loved to wear blond wigs lookin' like a complete buffoon would add her uninvited comments in. "Uh-huh, ain't nah reason fo' hur to be dat dang big. What's wrong wit' dem folks. Don't dey know she gonna have heart trouble. Mark my words." She'd point her index finger and shake it like she was slicing up that poot she just let loose. "All dat fat git aroun' her heart, then what dey gonna do?" She'd hum like she was singing in the Missionary choir. And once she got started it was hard to get her to shut up. On and on she would go. "Dat's what's wrong wit' us Black folks now, we's always waitin' till the last minute to git it right. We's love to procrashinates." (She could never say the word procrastinates.) 'But as soon as the doctor say something wrong wit' us. Oh, we wanna cry fo' Jesus.'" She'd show those butter-colored teeth like they were sparkling white, twist her big black and pink lips and fold her arms like a chill had crawled up it. All that blubber used to just swing back and forth, back and forth. I always used to wonder if aunt Gird was in the circus with the lions and tigers and bears. Oh my, aunty Gird was the ugliest aunty I'd ever seen. God, forgive me but it was so true. Then my evil aunt Priscilla—the mental case in our family. Aunt Priscilla was mean and nasty for no apparent reason. She weighed about three hundred pounds with mosquito bite sized titties and a flat pancake ass. And she never shaved under her armpits. Eew! Nasty. I think she mighta been born evil in her momma's womb. I swear I do. I never saw her smile, not once. Everyone in the family kept her at a distance. No one ever tried to double-cross her because we knew that her type of payback would kill you with kindness, if you know what I mean. With two husbands D.O.A and cause of death being "natural" no one played with Aunt Priscilla.

The bitch was psychotic.

Growing up, I always felt Aunt Priscilla was a little weird. All of a sudden, Aunt Priscilla thinks she's a lesbo. She took it as far as trying to pick skanks up off the block. I still believe Aunt Priscilla got more than a few screws loose. Yet she had the gull to be talkin' about me as if I was hopeless. "Oh…well, honey chile, you gotta die some day might as well eat what you want. Eat chile, eat. Ain't nothin' wrong wit' a little meat on those bones of yours?" And she'd brush her callous palm against my cheek, scratching my flawless skin and then laugh out loud like a demented crackhead. My eyes would wander from aunt to aunt unaware that they were making a mockery of me.

During the summer my aunt Maddy with her high yellow West Virginian complexion, over processed hair, and full-figure frame who loved to flash her 24-karart gold bangles around would come to visit from down South with her husband uncle Willie. Aunt Maddy would kneel down on her bad knee, and squeeze both of my cheeks 'cause she said they felt like squishy balls. She probably needed some dick. Then she'd giggle and pinch 'em so much that it made my face numb. "This chile just as healthy as can be. Wha' y'all feedin' her?" She'd asked, waiting for a response from anyone who was listening. I just stood there lookin' around all dumbfounded as drool dribbled down my finger and onto my Jackson Five T-shirt. Then uncle Willie with his four-eyed self, husky voice and buck-tooth all covered in deep dark skin would chime in. "Naw, that's just baby fat. She'll drop down in size as she gets older." Daddy with subtlety would meddle his two cents in. "Now, sis, you two stop hovering over my baby. That's my baby." He'd smile and chuckle to soften his words, but he meant every word of it. And I'd smile feeling like Daddy was protecting me from the grown-up spooky monsters.

I was Daddy's gem, not his favorite. He didn't show favoritism. He loved my sister, Bernetta and me equally. Neither got more than the other. Daddy easily took offense when folks talked about me, though. That troubled him for some unknown reason. I never asked any questions I was just glad that he cared so much. Daddy was my biggest motivator because he had traveled my journey of being big-boned stemming from his childhood. He said his daddy called him "Chubby" as a nickname. He said that he never took offense because he knew that his father loved him to death. Since Daddy shared that story with me I felt he understood what I was going through. He knew how to soothe nurturing ointment all over me.

Every mornin' before Daddy left for work he'd pinch my cheeks and call me *precious, special,* and *beautiful.* I'd smile with hardly any teeth in my mouth, stick my pinky in it, and slobber all over it as drool dribbled down my hand onto my raggedy pink I Love Lucy T-shirt. I would just smile and slobber. Daddy always knew how to make me feel good about myself, even when no one else would, especially Mama.

As I grew, Mama had her own way of saying things to me. She'd normally say, "Chocolate, you *could* be so pretty if..." "If only you *would*" or "Maybe you *should*..." I would start walking away before she even finished her sentence. I'll admit it was kinda rude but her words were very abrasive and I didn't know if she even realized it or stopped to think before she spoke. After a while of hearing her bashes, I simply tuned her out. I'd look her straight in the face, act like I was listening and distracted my mind with something worthwhile. Her words really hurt me. I didn't have anyone else who understood, but Daddy. A girl like me needed encouragement to carry me through, not criticism from Mama.

Mama was brainwashed by Granny. She was taught that being thin, slim, and trim was the happening thing, back in her days. Granny convinced her of that as a teen. She said being overweight was taboo and it would lead her down a road to nowhere in corporate America 'cause most people were looking for beauty, physique, and intellect. I called it the Triple Threat. She said if you're lacking especially when it came to body frame you might as well call it a day 'cause no one would even acknowledge you standing there.

Mama somehow managed to corrupt Bernetta's mind with that nonsense. But I didn't feed into it for a minute. I wasn't buying into it because it would only mess my head up. I have enough issues. I would be a lost cause if I believed Mama. I have to confess though; Mama was blessed with good looks and a trim fit body. She's one of those lucky ones but I often wonder why she keeps nagging me.

Quite often I think she is a bit obsessed with weight. I believe that she feels that I should look and be like her. But I'm not. I'm me. And it just so happens to be that I'm the spitting image of my dad.

Not to get all religious and whatnot, but I often question the Man upstairs motives. I shouldn't, but I do. I wonder why He did this to me. Yeah. What nerve! *Thank you, God, for piling me up with all this weight.* But then I think about it for a split second and realize He doesn't put the food in my mouth. I do. He doesn't make me chew it. I do. He doesn't make me swallow it. I do. I guess I should be grateful that I was born a healthy child. A little too healthy, if you ask me.

Deep inside I am resentful because I don't look like the other twelve, thirteen, fourteen, and fifteen-year-old girls in the teen magazines or at school. I don't even look like the girls on the commercials with skin that's flawless and supple, posing in their slim frames. Have you ever seen a big girl in a commercial trying to sell something? Okay, a bra. Okay, maybe Queen Latifah for her makeup line of *Cover Girl Queen Collection*. But was she in the commercial at my age? No. At least I've never seen her in one. I have no one to even idolize. I just look like...um...I'm still thinking. I can't even compare myself to anyone.

It's not my fault...that's what I keep telling myself. I push the blame elsewhere. My first target is skinny people. They are mean to me so it is only fair to blame 'em. I didn't think it would be so painful being meaty. Daddy never told me any stories of him being picked on. *Maybe I need to ask him*. Skinny people are ignorant by staring like they never seen a big girl before. It only makes matters worse for me. They don't know what I am going through and they don't care to know. They are downright nasty. I hear 'em snickering behind my back. Some are just insensitive and do it right in front of my face or on my way home from school. And these are grown-ups. Uh-Huh. I expect it from kids my age. Nonetheless, it hurts. It doesn't seem to matter to them that their cruelness hinders me. I guess they think it is comical to hurt my feelings. As if to say, "Her skin is thick, she won't feel a thing." They're wrong because I do feel it. I have inner scars to prove it.

I have a complex from all their jokes. My self-esteem lowered to the point that I feel ugly to anyone's eyes. It's sad. I'm sad. But I comfort myself with thinking about all the things my dad had done for me. It cost him much money to try to gloss me up. He purchased *Neutrogena*, and *Queen Helene's Oatmeal 'n Honey Natural Facial Scrub*, *Queen Helene's Green Mask Jubilee*, and *Witch Hazel* for an astringent. I've visited several dermatologists who prescribed skin care medication that seem to worsen my condition before it improved. To me, it would have been less painful if they'd just stroked my ego and then released some kind words to comfort me. But they didn't. Instead they kindly took my dad's hard-earned money and slipped it in their pockets.

One evening while watchin' TV an infomercial catches my attention, *Proactiv*, and Daddy ordered it on a 30-day trial basis. It actually helped my acne-prone skin and faded my blemishes. I had fewer breakouts. But Daddy couldn't keep up with the two-month automatic debits from his checking account and I had to go back to my old regimen: soap and water.

As far as my weight, I drink *Slim Fast* and hope for the best. Eat a *Lean Cuisine*, but I still be hungry. Daddy even took me to a nutritionist in Bremerton Square, a quiet city a few miles from DeWitt. People from DeWitt call it the Hicksville mainly because they rarely see a black person walking down the street. The landscape of Bremerton Square is manicured green lawns, high-rise buildings, no litter on the grounds, nice big parks, big houses with driveways that stretch out long and wide, and lots of fancy cars, and snooty-looking women dressed in the finest of designer wear. I always envied how they lived. Well, the nutritionist, a white woman with brunette hair that flowed down her mid-back. She is a hefty looking woman—not slender, not fat, kinda neutral. She walks out of her office and introduces herself as Mizzy Matherson. Daddy stands in her presence and they shake hands while I kinda stare her down. I am marveling that big ass rock on her ring finger. There I go drifting in thought of when I'll have a ring just like that, if not bigger on my ring finger. Mizzy invites us into her small office. I sit in the cushiony yellow chair, while Daddy sits on the couch while Mizzy sits beside me in a black leather chair. She cuts to the chase and asks Daddy some questions about me as if I am not even sitting there. Each time Daddy responds she cuts her eyes over at me and jots down something on white paper that is slightly hidden in a manila folder. I remain quiet. As Daddy pauses from rambling on and on Mizzy closes her manila folder and looks at Daddy and me coming to this useless conclusion. "Mr. Tease, um, when your daughter gets stressed, she eats. And when she eats, she suffers. Obviously, your daughter suffers from depression." Even I knew that. Well, Daddy and I came to the conclusion that Mizzy Matherson was a complete dipstick. She wasn't worth our time or money.

When my mind plays tricks on me I take the easy way out and blame other people, mostly skinny chicks for my predicament. They bother me 'cause they walk around like it's all about them. *Enough already!* They come out here strutting around shooting the breeze wearing those skimpy little skirts, halters, hip-huggers, and tight fitted jeans that suffocate their crotches. Uh-Huh. *Oh, they make me sick!* Don't they momma's tell them that wearing tight jeans creates yeast infections? I am hatin' on 'em. But...but...I have good reason 'cause being big-boned is no picnic. And even though I envy them I still have cravings for food. Like I can go for a turkey and Swiss cheese and tomatoes, lettuce, pickles, olives, oil and vinegar with extra mayo sandwich right about now.

The boys in the neighborhood jokingly poke fun of me, at least I make it seem like it's jokingly, but realistically they mean every word that spews out of their mouths. I smirk to cover what I am really feeling inside—empty. I've been doing this for so long that it's become a natural reaction. I guess that's why I admire Mo'nique from the movie *Precious* so much. I mean she's gettin' paid big n' all. It seems in real life she doesn't seem to care about what people think of her. She just oozes confidence. She uses her plus size in a comical way I guess to take the sting off. I do the same thing, but it doesn't lessen the low blows that I give to myself. See, when Mo'nique mocks her weight it doesn't appear to hurt as much. I wonder how she manages to smile, though. Is it part of her rehearsal? Or is it real? I wonder did she feel like crying underneath because of the pressure. Then I thought about if she was always a big girl stemming from her childhood on up, like me. How it affected her in life? Obviously, she seems to have overcome any type of low self-esteem. At least, that's how it appears on TV.

My life is totally different. I live in misery behind closed doors. I try to hide it on my face on the outside and most of the time I feel like a fake. Why can't I just be me? It isn't that simple. I wish it was but I feel so much pressure that I can't even handle it majority of the time. And the pressure grows and grows until I lose control and eat…just because. I have many, many reasons why I eat but I have no outlet. So, I hibernate in my bedroom, eating junk food that I have hidden in my closet, underneath my bed, and dresser drawers. I hide candy bars in my socks for those lonely, self-pity parties. It soothes me when I am feeling down. It's my pick me up. Then around 7:30 in the evening, Mama calls everyone for dinner and I clean my plate as if I am hungrier than a dog. After all that junk food I still have room in my stomach to finish a whole meal, plus have seconds. *Man, I got it bad.*

I walk into the living room; sit down to watch a little TV while having a snack of chocolate chip cookies and a pint of vanilla ice cream. Then I take a shower around nine o' clock, and head for bed, but before I lay my head down I nibble on a Snicker bar and brush my teeth, and then fall asleep.

Come morning I take a shower, get dressed, and head for the kitchen 'cause I'm starvin'. I can smell Ma's pancakes and sausages. I say, "Good morning," to my parents, sit down, and pile my plate with about eight pancakes, tablespoon of butter on each one, saturate them with Maple syrup, and add about eight link sausages on my plate. I say grace and dig in. After I eat, I wash my food down with two eight-ounce glasses of whole milk. And then leave for school.

Everyday I meet up with my crew: Eccentric McFadden (205 lbs. Height: 5'4"), Titty Symon (201 lbs. Height: 4'11"), and Mosquito Bite (200 lbs. Height: 5'2"), and as for myself, I am a whooping (210 lbs. Height: 5'5"). They're my girlfriends. My girlfriends and I crave the skinny life. We're all big for our ages, but we made a pact that we won't always be these sizes. A lot of times we laugh and chant in unison, "Its baby fat!" Yeah. But deep down it hurts to be soooo big.

August is here so quickly. Back to school shopping is making Eccentric, Mosquito, and me go crazy trying to shop for the latest fashion at Lane Bryant, Payhalf, and Ashley Stewart. It is important that we look our best because we are entering high school. We are going to be freshmen and we are excited. We all had stayed on track with our daily exercise and each of us has lost ten pounds a piece. We deserve to be on our shopping spree.

I stand in the fitting room marveling myself in the mirror as I try on a pair of trousers and a long sleeve button down shirt. It's an extra treat to be shopping here because Eccentric gets her discount so neither Mosquito nor I pay full price because she put us down as her immediate family. I bought about four outfits. Mosquito bought about three. And Eccentric bought about five, and she also bought a pair of boots from Baker's shoes. Then we head home.

Mama is sitting in the living room with the phone in her hands making some annoying sound when I walk in the house. Her eyes are glossy with streaks of tear marks running down her face. She seems in a daze of some sort.

"Mama?"

She doesn't move.

"Mama?"

I slowly remove the phone out of her hand and sit it in its cradle. Mama turns and looks at me with pain in her eyes.

"Yo, yo, yo, daddy and sister…" she completely loses it. She bawls on the floor right in front of me.

"Mama, what?"

Her hands pound the carpet, hard. "Why, whyyyyyyyyyyyy!"

And then she says it loudly; your Dad and Bernetta were killed in a car accident—hit by a drunk driver!!!

My body starts to shake. "I wanna see Daddy!" I scream at the top of my lungs. "Lemme see Daddy!!!! I want my DADDY!!"

Mama gasps for air as her right hand clenches her chest. "You can't, Chocolate." she stares at me with bloodshot red eyes.

"Why not!!!!!!" I say in a crackling voice of agony. I fall to my knees bawling my eyes and heart out.

"Because...I was told that their bodies were burnt beyond recognition." Mama says trying to give a reasonable explanation in a raspy voice of anguish.

"DADDY, DADDY, DADDY!!!!" I scream until my voice grows hoarse.

That day my whole world comes crumbling down. Mama ends up putting the house up for sale. We move into an apartment on Ennis Avenue, still in DeWitt. Mama couldn't spend another day in that house. It reminded her too much of Daddy and Bernetta. Funny how life just sweeps everything you've ever loved right from under your feet. I have no problem losing weight now especially at the wake, which is held at Augusta Mitchell's Funeral Home, but it really hit me hard, hard at the funeral. Daddy and Bernetta have closed caskets and they are buried in the family plot at Serenity Cemetery in Claxton, which is actually five miles from our old residence. I have to say good-bye to the only man who accepts me for me—my daddy. *Who am I gonna have to talk to now?* Mama? Yeah aiight. I wish I had been buried with Daddy and Bernetta just to stop the pain.

***

Ennis Avenue

Today is a day of devastation for me, Chocolate Tease. A day I wished I could change with a blink of an eye, but unfortunately, I can't. *It's too late*, I think to myself. I have a little person growing inside of my thirteen and a half year old frame. It is scary. So scary that I take baby breaths each time I think about it. *I am with child. Me.* I shake my head from side to side, still in disbelief. It just...just happened. Well, not exactly. I mean I allowed this to happen to me. That's more adult-like. At least, it sounds more adult-like.

My cognac-colored eyes fill with emotion. My face is a face of distress. And my thick frame is a body of nerves. *What am I gonna do?* I can't even respond back to myself. It is that complicated. I heave, staring at an image of how my life was just a month or two ago. I am a straight B student striving to get A's. All I want is to

25

make mama proud maybe then she'll cut me some slack.

I take baby steps traveling home. Slowly and cautiously, I walk light on my feet, not to disturb the little one growing inside of me. She or he is probably snoozing away. I walk up the busy and congested streets of Ennis. All I see is debris, abandoned buildings with gang symbols, high grass that resembles cornfields, dirtiness, bums, junkies hanging on the corner talking about nothing while sipping on alcohol disguised in brown paper bags. All I hear is cussing and fussing. Thugs sitting on the block scoping people out to rob. Little babies sit in their strollers crying up a storm 'cause they're hungry while mommies too busy getting her habit stroked. I see this day after day and it makes my heart hurt. I happen to take a glance to my right and I see other girls around my age. Boy, do they look free. Free from what I am currently experiencing, me being with child and all. What is mama gonna think of me, I wonder.

I arrive at my brick building and my right hand pulls the door handle back as my pink Timberland boots head in the lobby. As soon as I walk in I notice the elevator has a sign plastered upon it in bold letters: Out-of-Order. Shoot, I say to myself. I walk upstairs. Three floors. I huff, a little annoyed. After each flight of steps I feel a throbbing sensation in my legs. Like pins tingling. My palms are itchy and achy. My nipples are tender to the touch, and my breasts feel like two water jugs. I feel a bit winded. And my heart is beating extremely hard and fast. As I get closer to the third floor, I feel this sick feeling in my stomach. Almost like butterflies or flies, I can't tell which. I feel anxious. Overwhelmed with guilt and frustrations.

Once on my floor, I hesitate to move. I am afraid to move forward for whatever reason. The hall is long, quiet, and slightly dark. It has a scent of food cooking. What kind? I don't know. I can smell it and it is making me nauseous. I lean against the heavy door and swallow back down this watery spit in my mouth. I feel like I want to vomit, but I don't. I just feel like I want to. I stare briefly into space. Well, 'nough time for me to revisit the scene in my head.

Kommon Jamison, the six-foot, athletic jock with light skin and hazel eyes is all I can think about. I'm sayin' he's the most popular boy in school, mainly because his family is somewhat well off because they live in the suburbs of Bohemia, but he is temporarily staying with a relative so that is how he is able to attend Joss High School.

Kommon is the kind of boy who likes to showboat his fancy ride (a mustang) and all the girls be sweating him. The ladies man who I assumed was just *my* man. That was a slap in the face when I witnessed with my very own eyes him walking arm-to-arm with Samantha Smith—she's every boys dream girl. I tried to compose myself, and I did, as I watched them stroll down the hallways like I never existed. All of my fellow classmates watched. It was sooooo humiliating.

Them two makes me sick to my stomach. And little did I know around that time was the signs or symptoms of "life" growing inside of me. But confirmation was when my white/black girlfriend, Spring Fever, approached me with the idea that possibly I could be walking around with child and not knows it. If she never stuck her nose in my business I would've never sought to find out. The sleepiness. Morning sickness. Emotions ran rampant. Weight gain as well as my little "friend" not visiting for nearly two months was a dead giveaway that something is wrong. *Did I really want to know?* No. I was living in denial, but once I got home that evening I look myself in the full-length mirror in mama's bedroom…something began to show. Tears fill my eyes. My body quivers in my skin. Here I am almost fourteen. My birthday is coming and I have to deal with this happening to me! *What is mama gonna say?* Honestly, I dread the thought of finding out.

Mrs. Gracie Tease, tall, raisin-colored complexion woman with fine long good hair is a hardworking security guard. She's been employed with APP Securities for a couple of years. She loves serving the public, especially at School 110. She adores children, but she is not and has not entertained the thought of becoming a young grandmother no time soon. The forty-three year old woman hasn't even thought of engaging in conversation about sex with me. It is the farthest from her mind. In her eyes, I am a good girl—a wholesome girl. A virgin, still locked in her cocoon. I, now being the only child, Gracie have high expectations for me. Since I've always exceeded her expectations since kindergarten, the last thing Gracie would think of would be for me to be engaging in sexual intercourse. Little does she know the agony is buried in my chest and reality is diligently growing inside of my once little girl's tummy.

Still leaning against the heavy door, I am paranoid to take another step. Dreading to see mama's face. Afraid she might be home early since she is starting her two weeks vacation, today. That's good for her but timing sucks for me.

My pink Timberland boots feel like lead is weighing me down. The guilt is that heavy on my soul as I stand in front of door 3D, a bit lightheaded. I pull out my keys from my lightweight jacket pocket with Mickey Mouse dangling from my keychain and insert the key and twist the lock until I hear it click. I gently turn the knob and walk into a world of remembrance of when I was just a girl. But that soon changed with each month that life is growing like rose petals. I used to be a bud, but now I am blooming into teen-mother.

I huff a heavy sigh, anticipating the worst to come. Then, the phone rings and I immediately jump out of my skin. Girlllllll, I think to myself. Then, proceed to walk into the kitchen and lift the wall-mounted phone and say, "Hel-lo," with my eyes cutting from side to side.

"Hello. May I speak with Mrs. Tease, please?" A woman with a Hispanic accent asks.

Immediately, tears begin to build in my eyes. The voice sounds most familiar, as it is Mrs. Felix.

"Um, Mrs. Felix, my moms not home yet." I say.

"Oh. Hi Chocolate. Be sure to tell her to call me at Planned Parenthood, okay."

"Ah…ah…yes, ma'am." I stutter nervously as my long lashes bat back the tears that are dying to roll down my face. I am beyond terrified. Yet I try with all of my might to calm myself down. "Um, I'll do that."

Mrs. Felix's voice sounds muffled as if she has her hand over the receiver. Then I hear her say, "tell her I'll call her back in a few minutes," to whomever she is talking to.

"Chocolate."

"Yes."

"Sorry about that. I'm trying to do two things at once."

I crack a smile by her demeanor. She is a nice lady.

"Okay. Well, have your mother call me ASAP (as soon as possible). As I've discussed with you, since you are a minor I have to inform your mother of your test results."

I bow my head in shame, and pat my thick thigh with my clammy fingers. "Um, I know. You told me."

"You still have my card, right?"

"Yes, ma'am."

"Be sure to tell her to call me."

"I will."

"Chocolate."

"Yes, ma'am."

"Don't worry. When you worry your baby worries."

There is the proof that I dread to hear. I am indeed with child.

We hang up.

I feel like crawling in the closet and never coming out. *What will mama think of me? What have I done with my life? How could I have been so st-u-pid!*

Calm down, Chocolate, I say to myself. *I might as well calm down now 'cause when mama finds out she is going to chew in my hide.*

To make a long story short, Mrs. Felix gets in contact with Mama, and boy does she let me have it with her foul tongue? It literally takes her about a month to look at me and another week and a half to speak to me. After she cools down, we have a long, long, long talk about my options. I end up having the baby but I can't financially take care of her. And mama can't afford the extra burden of another mouth to feed so I decide to give the baby up for adoption. Well, that's what we decided. Mama is trying her best to care for me after the death of Dad and Bernetta. It is difficult, but we have no choice but to start our lives over.

Kommon stopped speaking to me and I move on with my life. Kommon ends up having a baby or shall I say babies with Paige Kendall. She is that "jump off" in school, if you know what I mean.

By the end of my freshman year, Kommon has about six kids by several different baby mommas. And I am this girl that gave her baby up for adoption so that I could have a better life. It hurt me deeply. I hate Kommon with great passion mostly because he disregarded our child and me. Often I wonder how my baby is doing, but often I have to correct my thinking and remind myself that she's no longer my baby. Hopefully she's in a good home with loving parents.

WHUPP "D"

"Whupp can you take the garbage out for me?" Bottom asks in her baby voice. She always does that shit when she wants me to do something so that her big ass won't have to get up off the couch. The chick loves to watch TV. As I am heading out to the hallway my mind drifts thinking about my moms Bump. I miss her. Lupus took her away from me too soon. I open the door to the incinerator and a stench of piss hits my nose. I quickly throw the bag down the shoot and walk back into the house staring at what my life has become. If I could turn back the hands of time, I wonder if would I. "Dad-dy." I hear my youngest son say. He breaks my concentration. "Yeah, Lil' Man, whatchu want wit' daddy?" He just stands there looking all innocent wit' his droopy pamper damn near sagging off his little butt. I sniff in and that's all it takes to know what Lil' Man wants, damn, he shitted and needs to be changed. "C'mon, Lil' Man, c'mere." I say as I take his little chocolate-colored hand and reach in the box for a pamper and guide him into the bedroom to clean him up.

Everyday I question whether I made the right decision taking on this role of: Daddy. Everyday I find myself feeling like maybe I rushed into something because of obligation, not because of love.

***

I was raised in a single parent household in the 'hood of Ennis wit' my moms Bump D. Bump. We shared a one-bedroom on Auburn and Grover Street. This 'hood was notorious for high crime and homicides so I had to watch my back at all times.

Bump was everything to me. She played both roles as far as I was concerned. I respected her to the utmost. She was holding it down working at McDonald's on Cleaver and Montgomery as an overnight supervisor. She never got involved with another dude since pops. Big-Whupp attempted to come back but moms stopped him in his tracks before he could even start that bullshit gift of gab. She said, "Fucken nigga, I don't have time for games. If you don't wanna take care of your responsibilities, nigga don't. But don't come back here tryna get this ass. It ain't gonna happen. I don't know where the fuck you've been. You could be out here fucking these skanks for all I know. And you think that I am going to let you stick yo' dick in my pussy. Nigga, please, leave that dope alone 'cause it got yo' head all fucked up." After she shot him down in size I ain't seen him since. He ain't even show his face at the wake or funeral. Since he was a no-show I practically disowned the nigga. The way I saw it and the way I felt made it simple to say: I ain't got no father!

Yeah. Big-Whupp left when I was nine-years-old. He met some chick wit' a big ass and his mind got all discombobulated. Shit, I never knew *ass* could literally make a brotha' go crazy like that but it did wit' that joker. Some men have feet fetish. Tittie fetish. Hips fetish. Not that nigga. It was the ass. So, of course, I had to grow up faster than my years. No more *Scooby-Doo* drawers. No more *Roadrunner* cartoons. Nah. I had graduated to *Hanes* for men.

By twelve I had facial hair. Yeah. Bump kept tellin' me to shave. I kept saying, "what for its only going to grow back. Don't you know? I'm the man of the house." She'd chuckle. But I meant that shit. And since that day I filled the shoes, not in her crib but in my girl Bottom Up's crib.

Bottom was about 4'11" with a nice ass and some big bazooka titties. They were so big she could breastfeed a village and still have milk leftover. She got that flawless fudge-colored complexion with those come-and-get-me brown eyes of hers. She also got two small seeds: 3 (and he still ain't potty-trained), 5 (and he is by one of my cousins). Both baby daddies' were in the slammer. So yours truly had taken the driver's seat in that house. We resided in Hamp and Bennett Projects. This project was owned and operated by two big time drug-dealers who reformed their lives, after serving numerous years in prison. Matt Hamp and Kornell Bennett used to be the two most notorious street hustlers the city of DeWitt had ever conceived. They had the blocks locked with young girls dealing because they looked innocent. I mean who would've suspect a thirteen to seventeen year old teen-mother to be hustling drugs by stashing 'em in their baby strollers while their babies were in it. C'mon. Hamp and Bennett were brilliant in my eyes. It was an ingenious scheme those two masterminded. But one of 'em, (I think it was Hamp) who broke the code of tradition to not mix business with pleasure. Yeah, Hamp fell short and started fucking one of his dealers—her name was Mistakke Michele. And she was a beauty as far as looks and body. Man, Mistakke was sweet on the eyes. That girl was curvy, thick, with big ass titties, fat juicy ass all smothered in sugary brownness. She was fine as hell. None of the chicks around the way had shit on her. She was lovely.

Well, Mistakke got caught up wit' (white boy) Hamp and he got caught up wit' her and knocked her up, while Kornell (black dude) kept his eye on the prize: money. Shit got hot and heavy after that because Mistakke already had five kids at the age of seventeen and another mouth to feed was murder on her pockets even with the dough she was getting from her hustle. That's when the arguing started to erupt. Then out of the blue another chick came into the picture named Concentration Givens. Concentration was a nice piece of ass wit' no kids. Mistakke got pissed and blew the whistle on their lucrative operation. Yeah. They got raided. The cops confiscated all their shit. I'm more than sure the crooked ones pocketed some of that cash. I'm talking millions. Well, after Hamp and Bennett served their time they came back to their stomping grounds of DeWitt with a new attitude and new outlook on life. They both reinvented themselves by becoming partners again, but this time they got into the real estate game.

Hamp and Bennett projects were not my dream home, but it was, what it was, you feel me? *I'm da man in dis house.* I usedta say that shit all the time wit' my chest puffed out. That's what I usedta say. But real talk, huh. I wore a tight face most of the time. My pockets were filled with lint balls, but my feet were always laced in a new pair of the latest sneaks. I worked hard. I mean hard, but I didn't seem to be reaping any of the reward for my hard work. And that pissed me off.

I'm sayin', man, I usedta catch the train 5:30 a.m., and got off at 11:00 at night and didn't get home until midnight. And Bottom ain't cook shit! The chick only worked part-time so she had mad time to cook me a home cooked meal. A brotha' had no choice but to starve because everything in the fridge was frozen. Don't get me wrong we both did the food shopping, but the only way I got a consistent meal was if I did it my damn self. Fast food was Bottom's thing, not mine. Bump always cooked. This was some new shit that I wasn't tryna get usedta. Here I was 5'9" about 160 or less. Honey-toned. Not a bad lookin' brotha'. Actually I was handsome—an eye catcher to the ladies. One thing about me was that I never dated black chicks. Nah. My fetish was Puerto Rican chicks wit' a Buffi booty. Shit, I sound like that *dude*.

Now, Bottom was black. How da hell she snagged me? Well...you figure it out. Nah, nah, it was the Afro centric pussy. Nah, Bottom was there for me at a time when I needed someone. Yeah, during and after Bump died. Brotha' never forgot. So I couldn't do her dirty. Brotha' gotta heart—too big of a heart.

After a few weeks of being in her kids' presence, Bottom had her kids calling me Daddy. Hell, I felt like a father. Or maybe I thought it was all just pretend. Like I could leave at any given time and nobody would be affected by it. It wasn't that cut and dry. I found that out much later. It was too late to just bounce. Her kids needed me. They needed a father/daddy to role-play. I took those boys under my wing. Made sure they had food in the fridge, sneakers on their tiny feet, clothes on their backs, and toys for X-mas. And haircuts. I made sure they had clean clothes because I washed the clothes. Well, Bottom and I alternated weeks but I felt like I was at the Laundromat more than her. I was working full-time at a food market. Been there for two years. Plus, I was going to school part-time at the community college tryna better myself. You know, make myself more marketable for the job market. Yeah. Ok.

My hairline was receding by the time I turned 23. Actually it started receding at 19 or 20. That's around the time my distant brother on my father's side came into the picture. Young Bro got himself in some shit so Bottom took him in fo' a nigga. At the time I was livin' wit' Bump, but I had to jet because I needed and wanted my freedom. Shit, I was a man. If I wanted to smoke a blunt, I could with no questions axed. If I wanted to take a swig of Henny, I could. If I wanted to get my swerve on and fuck the shit outta Bottom havin' her scream my name (I chuckled), brotha' could. I had freedom. I was da man of da house!

I got hip to the deal real quick living wit' Bottom. I remember a time when Bottom axed me for some money and I told her no. I mean DAMN! Drain me dry woman! I'm sayin' I was taking care of business. My pockets stayed on "e" (empty) fuckin' wit' her. Man, I was ready to bounce for real. I mean all we did was argue over dumb shit. I tried to resolve shit and Bottom just had to have her way or she went ballistic. *This ain't no healthy environment for me or her kids.* That's right! Her kids! Brotha' head was coming out of the clouds. Fuck dis shit, I said to myself. Especially after Bottom axed to use my cell phone. I let her. You know, that chick had the audacity to disrespect a brotha' by calling some other nigga (in front of me) and axing him fo' some money. I blacked da fuck out. I mean BLACKED DA FUCK OUTTTTTTT! And before I dared put my hands on her, brotha' bounced out the door, but I didn't bounce out of her life. Nah. It wasn't that simple. I had a connection with those kids. I couldn't disappoint them. They had enough disappointments from men. I understood how it felt to want a father, and not have one. Man, those boys were strapped to my heart. All I kept hearing was Dad-dy. *I ain't dey Daddy.* I don't have kids. I was a single young man looking older than my years from stress. It was time to bounce.

See, I had my plan set. By the time I did my income tax I figured I'd use that money to jet. But to my surprise, Young Bro's mama decided she wanted to claim her son. She wasn't even livin' in

Jersey. She moved out of state on the sneak tip. Now, how da fuck could she claim him and I had been bustin' my ass to support him for a year and three months, huh?! That chick tried but eventually I got my four grand. This was my ticket out. But Bottom pulled a fast one on a brotha' wit' that pussy of hers. Yep. Brotha' was whipped!

I wasn't a hustler, thug-type, drug-dealer, or joker that went around robbing people for thrills. Nah. For one, I was a mommas-boy. I was a good cat. Came from a home of morals and values and struggles. I watched Bump do without many a days to provide for me. She couldn't give me the world, but damned if she didn't try to. I must admit, though, I gave her hell growing up. I guess I was rebellious because Big Whupp wasn't in my life. A young boy needed a father. I needed manly advice—a father's perspective on adolescent shit. I needed him to clown me on getting my first piece of pussy. You know, man shit. Us sitting around gossiping like women. Yeah, men gossip too. He'd joke about the "smell-my-finger" thing boys' do. Yeah. He'd lean back in his chair and say some shit like, "Do it smell like strawberries or peaches?" and I'd start giggling 'cause that's what young boys do. And I'd sniff my finger like a dumb ass to answer his question. And I'd say, "Nah. It smells like rotten fish." And he'd say, "Ah son, dat dirty bitch ain't wash her pussy." And I'd be like, "WORD!" And he'd be like, "Yeah man, I'm surprise your dick ain't fall off." And I'd be like, "WORD!" I peeked down below to make sure my boy D was still intact. So after knowing that D was straight Pops takes me under his wing and pussyeducates me. I kid you not I ain't wanna see, sniff, or fuck another *pussy* for weeks. Damn straight! From all the scents and shit: one smelled like cherry lollipop. One smelled like vinegar and water. One smelled like bouquet of flowers. And then one turned a brotha' out that smelled like chocolate. I mean that good shit too! After that one sniff I was hooked.

I searched that chocolate pussy down and had yet to find it. Around that time was when I wanted to leave Bottom. I'm sayin' when we met she was a sweet little thang. I had me a ready-made family. Yeah I thought I was da man. But I had taken over a role that wasn't mine to take. Don't get it twisted, Bottom tried to provide the best for her kids. Shit, single motherhood was a bitch, if you axed me. I didn't pity her because she was taken care of business to the best of her ability. But Bottom had a lot of shit wit' her. She could do all the wrong in the world and expected me to just accept it like I was some pushover, some punk-ass nigga. My momma didn't raise no damn fool! So we'd argue like a married couple. I swear I was so glad I never got that chick pregnant. Oh, brotha' woulda been chained and shackled to that bitch. She had a heart, but was spoiled rotten. That was her father's fault. And I guess she expected niggas who got involved wit' her to lavish her wit' Air-Force Ones and gettin' her nails did, and dat weave shit. I wasn't doin' it anymore. I mean, yeah, in the beginning you on the chase so whatever, you feel me? But whatever I did to catch her. Shittttt I was willing to release her. I had had it. I'm sayin' gimme something, knawmean? Lemme see that you could look like a feminine woman. Shit, wear a dress and high-heels and makeup and turn a brotha crazy. Keep my cock hard. Make me feel like da man. Why you always gotta be lookin' thuggish—rough and tough—and hard. Don't no man wanna be showboating his gurl lookin' like a 'hoodrat. Be out in the streets cussin' and fussin' like a damn fool. Man, oh man, if Bump was here she would've cussed Bottom out and told me to bring my black ass back home. But that was Bottom—straight up ghetto.

I'd do fo' the boys in a heartbeat 'cause they were innocent. They didn't ask to be born. And the niggas (including my cousin) who knocked her ass up should've realized that too. But not all men were men. Some still had a boy's mentality. And the boy often got caught up in the fast-paced life and windup locked up. Some nigga's did little time and others did a lifetime. But I was one of the "blessed" ones. I was never a follower, per say. Nah. Well, in one instance I was because my nose was still sniffin' fo' dat chocolate twat.

***

Friday. I am walking down the street minding my own business. I keep thinking about the little one that I had inside of me. Not paying attention as to where I am walking I bump into this guy—this cute guy. I've never seen him before. I swear it was like he appeared out of nowhere. He seems kind of weird, though. Yeah. I say weird because he sniffs me like a dog. Yeah. Sniffs. I can't believe he just did that to me.

I cut my eye and purse my lips. "Excuse me, but did you just sniff me?" my forehead crumples.

He chuckles.

"No seriously, did you?"

He has this perplex look on his handsome face. "What you wearing? You got on perfume or something?"

"No. I don't wear perfume because I have sensitive skin."

"So, what you got on?"

"Nothing, but soap." I say rather sarcastically.

"So, that's *you* smelling like that?"

"Smelling like what?" I sniff myself to see what he is talking about. I don't smell anything out of the ordinary.

"You don't smell that?" he asks.

"Smell what?"

"That."

"What!" I snap.

"I got what you need, sweetness."

"And what I need?"

"In due time, sweetness. In due time." he smugly says.

"How you gonna just change the subject like that?" I ask.

"Easy."

We just stare at each other for a few minutes.

"What's your name?"

"Why?"

"Just wanna know."

"Chocolate."

"Girl, stop playing and tell me your *real* name."

"My first name is Chocolate and my last name is Tease."

"So, you mean to tell me that your parents named you Chocolate Tease on purpose."

"Yeah."

"Now why would they do that to a sweet thang like yourself?"

"I dunno."

He stands still with this puzzling look on his face. "Chocolate, huh?"

"You asking me all these questions, what's your name?"

"My name is Whupp D. Twat."

I can't help but to laugh in his face.

"What's so funny?"

"You have the nerve to be picking on my name and your name is Whupp D. Twat."

We both burst out into laughter.

"Well, I gotta get going Whupp."

"Wait! When can I see you again? C'mon now don't do a brother dirty. Don't look at me like that. You think I'm bullshitting you. Nah. That ain't me. I'm different from these niggas out here. Give me a chance to see?"

I cut my eyes to the sky waiting for daddy's approval. The cloud moves right so I take that as a sign.

"Don't think too hard on it," he says.

"Okay. Here is my phone number. Don't call me after ten o'clock 'cause my mother will go ballistic."

"Gotcha. Oh, I gotcha, sweetness. I gotcha."

***

The Loo-Loo Motel

Whupp massaged his crotch area with my favorite oil "Black Coconut" that he bought from this street entrepreneur named J. J was a longtime friend of Whupp's. J was Muslim. They usedta live in Hamp and Bennett Projects together. If I had to describe J I would say he was short. He kinda reminded me of Sammy Davis Jr., with his slender-frame and his mahogany-colored skin. He wore wire-framed glasses that made him look studious. He stood out like a sore thumb because his unique look was his burnt-orange colored beard. J was smooth with his hustle. I liked him. I mean he seemed like good people. He worked his hustle on Osborne Boulevard selling oils, soaps, oil burners, and home fragrances like kokomango--that's where Whupp spotted him. He bought the five-dollar bottle and then we went on our way, which was to the motel.

"Make love to it, baby. Mmmm. Damn, Twat, that's it, baby. Pacify that muthafuker. Oooh!" (*Whupp nicknamed me Twat because he said that he knew that one day he would marry me.*) I thought it was a bunch of bullshit. You know how it goes during steamy sex. That's fuckin' talk. It doesn't mean shit!

"Damn, Twat. Shittttttttt." Whupp slurred out his words with those perfectly shaped lips of his. His honey-toned body sprawled so relaxed across the motel's king-sized bed.

My tongue and lips made sound effects of popping and sucking as I pacified his cock in the quiet of night.

Slop. Pop. Slop. Pop. Slop.

"That's right, baby, pacify that muthafucker. Own that shit. Own it, baby." He moaned feeling the pleasure I was delivering. I was feeding him good. I had that nigga sprung. Whatever he wanted in bed I never deprived him. Never. I knew how to keep a nigga: feed and fuck him reallllll good. Whupp left hand gripped the top of my head, motioning it to go down to the root and suck his cock harder.

And I did.

"Oooh! Damn, Twat, you keep sucking my dick like this shit you ain't never gotta worry 'bout me cheating on you. Oh, shhhhhhhhhhhhhhhhhhhhhhhhhhhiiiiiiiittttt!"

Quite frankly I didn't believe him. I was going with the flow. Whupp was incapable of containing himself while I had ole boy in my mouth. I mean I gave great head. His brown eyes started rolling in back of his head. His soft lips pressed together as if he had been eating filet mignon. That shit felt sooooo fuckin' good to him. His arms spread wide. He wouldn't move a muscle. I had control. And I loved it. His dick tasted like white chocolate. Mmmm. I had Whupp feeling like he was on cloud nine. Like he'd just won the lottery. I had that nigga believing he was a millionaire. Yeah. I knew how to add the sugar on. That's right. I'd gas that nigga's head up. It wasn't talk, though. I meant every word. Whupp was sexy as hell to me. He turned me on. I wanted my baby to know that I was feelin' him strong. I'd fuck and suck no other's dick as long as I was happy. The operative word was *happy*.

Whupp's smooth legs spread even wider as my slimy wet tongue glided up and down, twist around the bulging head, and then slid back down mouthing his entire dick in one scoop. I had hot saliva oozing from my mouth like sticky sugarcane running down to his balls. I couldn't leave them out so I slouched down and gently licked 'em and sucked and slobbered 'em up. Whupp was pulling on the sheets. Then I rose back up and hid all six and a half inches of his manhood in my mouth. I suctioned that nigga hard. Then I'd get on top of him and rode him until a gush of wetness streamed from my pussy. I never knew I could cum like that. Yeah. Whupp was my heart. I was cumming hard fucking him. Hard. Whupp usedta love me down. I usedta be open. I mean widddddddeeeeeee open for dat nigga. I usedta love that nigga more than Michael Jackson so you know I was sprung. Yeah. That was that young naïve love.

By the time we graduated high school and before we were to head off for college Whupp proposed. And I accepted. I called Mama and asked if she'd be my witness and she said yes. A week or so later we went to the justice of peace at the DeWitt Municipal Complex downtown DeWitt. Whupp grew up with this Puerto Rican cat named Frugal Sanchez, a jet-black haired, short dude who spoke broken English in Hamp and Bennett Projects too. Frugal pronounced us as husband and wife. It was now official. I was definitely Whupp's… Chocolate Twat.

After marriage we rented an apartment for a few years and set a plan for Whupp to go to school full-time gaining his degree in architecture. I worked full-time and took night classes. With sixty or more credits I landed a job at the Board of Social Services in Bohemia, New Jersey. After graduating Phi Beta Kappa Whupp gained a prestigious position as an Architectural Engineer at The Isley Group, one of the largest and most lucrative architectural firms in the world. Thereafter, we built our first home in the suburbs of Bohemia.

TWAT

I'ma tell you how I *really* snagged Whupp to put that ring on my finger.

Well, one day I was listening to Notorious B.I.G CD and something he said piqued my interest so I decided to see if Whupp had the balls to do it.

"Whupp, I want you to shit on me and then fuck the shit outta me."

Whupp looked at me like I was crazy. "Are you serious?"

Next thing I knew the muthafucker really fell in love. And he's been shitting on me ever since I was in my late fifties. But somewhere in between all the shittin' Whupp got constipated. He might've needed some of that Dr. Miller's Iaso Tea this dark-skinned Muslim named Nyne tried to sell him last week. Whupp wouldn't budge. Anyway, I got wit' a new program.

***

The madness in my mind keeps rewinding and fast-forwarding, and then it stops after that last blow. POP! I can feel the stinging sensation above my right eye. Blood slowly oozing and crooked lining down my swollen face. I know by morning it will be black and blue. Good thing I bought that new foundation to cover his *love* for me. He loves me so much that he senselessly beats me. Sometimes I'm unrecognizable. He beats me till I crumble like stale bread. There I lay like a crumb, sickened. Where had I gone? How did I get involved in this? Why can't I leave? That's simple to answer. He won't let me go. He doesn't want me anymore; yet, he enjoys punishing me for things that are not right in his life. I'm blamed for him not having enough money. I'm blamed for him not finding a job. I'm blamed for him not getting that promotion. I'm blamed for him not waking up on time. I'm blamed for him not having what he needs. Shit, I'm blamed for him having a hole in his sock. I'm blamed for the ring around his shirt collar. For him wearing his brown shoes instead of black shoes. His dinner not being ready when he called to say that he wasn't coming home. Yet, he's telling me that he's hungry. I'm blamed for not being able to think like him. I'm not him! I'm blamed for every stupid thing that happens in his life. I'm blamed and then I'm used as his punching bag to let out his frustrations. There are 365 days out of the year. And everyday, unless it's a Wednesday, which is hump day (sex) I am beaten. And sometimes during sex I'm beaten if I don't want to give him head or if I don't fuck him hard enough. I'm smacked around in bed. That's not romantic. I'm only human. I'm supposed to be his woman, his wife, his friend, yet he treats me like dirt. And he expects me to suck his dick every time he waltzes in the door. C'mon. He has literally taken every part of me and abused it. He bashes me everyday. He cuts me with his unfeeling words. And every time my feet hit the door that's when the charming man I first met reappears. And once I fall for those bullshit lines that's when the smacks, slaps, upper cuts, fractured ribs, busted lips, blackened eyes, befriend me once again. I'M TIRED! And every time I pack my bags and walk out the door he finds me. He threatens me with death. And what do I say, "Well, dammit go ahead and kill me 'cause I am already dead, muthafucker!" And then he looks at me all dumbfounded and shit like I said something wrong. And to make matters worse he cheats on me. Then he wants to have sex with me. No. You are not going to infect me with the "package." This ain't no package deal. And he literally laughs in my face. He doesn't love me. And you wanna know something I don't love my damn self because if I did, I wouldn't be here. Dammit! I got some serious issues. I have a man who loved me, and I left because he could not fulfill my sexual needs. Whupp was a kind man. He never hit me in his life. And if he knew the things that I am putting up with with this man he would probably stop breathing.

You maybe wondering how the hell did this get so damn complicated? Well, for one I just lied. I wasn't getting my ass beaten. Nah. Twat was beating da ass. That's right! I fucked Whupp up for fucking around. That's right! I found out that he let some bitch suck his dick a long, long time ago. I ain't wanna hear shit! Okay. I blacked da fuck out and let a nigga know that I ain't nobody to fuck wit'. I will lay a nigga out in a heartbeat. And that's exactly what I did to Whupp. Laid dat nigga out wit' one punch. P-P-POW! I know. I let my emotions get in the fuckin' way for the one I love. A bitch tried, but Whupp pissed me off.

***

I snuggle under the heavy quilt in *my* king-sized bed and *turn off the lights.*

Turn that damn music off! Whupp, Whupp...Whupp, stop smooching with the ladies and listen? Why don't you light a fuckin' candle once in a blue afternoon? Huh? If they only knew the shit I gotta put up with your tired ass. Women wouldn't be flocking at your feet. Practically throwing their stinky ass panties in your face. If those bitches only knew. I'm supposed to be your woman, right? Right Whupp, yet you keep sharing my love with these hookers out here. I am tired of this bullshit. You hear me, Whupp? Whew, Lord. I'm so tired.

Listen here, what I am about to say may or may not speak for all women, but I am tired of being poked and stroked with your smooth talking lyrics. I need to flow like an abrupt thunderstorm. Yes, burst outside of myself, Whupp. I might as well get right down to it.

See, you may have forgotten but I have had plenty of dicks before you. Uh-huh. Different varieties. Sizes. Widths. You name it. I've had it. But you wanna know what I have never had? I never had a dick that talked to me. I'm talkin' about a bilingual dick. Yes, that speaks fluently in two languages. A man that can read my mind— read my body language to know when I need him to fuck me. Okay, that might've been a bit harsh, but that is how I am feeling at the present moment. I'm burning up, Whupp. No. I don't have a fever. I'm burning up because I need to relieve myself. Spitz these juices out of me! Okay, I'm stressed. And no, I don't nor have I ever owned, borrowed ('cause that's just nasty) a vibrator. I have my own personal vibrator—my middle finger I call Pistol-Whipped. That baby knows how to make my hole sing in soprano, but I want to sing from a dick, not my finger. Why can't you make me sing, Whupp?

41

Why? Why can't you of all men make my pussy sing?

Listen Whupp; I'm stressed because I am experiencing a condition called "Why Can't I Cum Muthafucker!!!"? It is a condition where two bodies joined as one are not communicating sexually. You know, deaf people communicate with sign language, right? So why is it a problem when it comes to sex? Don't shrug your shoulders. Answer me?! Hypothetically speaking, Whupp, this is how I see it for us women. See, your man is on top of you in missionary position, doggy-style or any position, for that matter, and your woman's mind wanders off, thinking. Why and what is she thinking about? Well, her attention span might've drifted because she is not feeling spontaneity, excitement, fireworks, or grenades. It's something missing. S, s, s, ...something that her man is not giving her. But what she feels she's getting is merely a boring fuck. Yes, a boring fucks, Whupp. So she finds herself thinking while he's humping the shit outta her. Now, she is not going to express to him how she truly feels about his lazy fuck. Heck, no! She is merely going to take the long ride down south and back. So during her traveling she is thinking about washing the dishes, doing the laundry, finishing that last chapter of a good read, work, shopping, lyrics to a song, dinner, polishing her toenails, something other than him humping and pumping her like a horny dog. Now, she's wondering where had the romance gone? She looks deep into his eyes trying to figure it out while his face is all contorted because he is about to cum, yet she has yet to climax. I know, I know, Whupp, it sounds fucked-up, but this is the way it is for some women, and truthfully I am fed the fuck up too. Okay. That hypothetical was about you, Whupp. I didn't want to hurt your feelings but damn baby can you at least try to pop my cherry?

Listen, I have all of this "juice" built up in me and I can't seem to find the right dick to make it rain. Yes, I've been job hunting. I'm telling you now because I can't do this anymore. I have needs just like you. And my needs are not being met. Whupp, my pussy wants to cry, sob uncontrollably, slobber out its frustrations, and I can't. Why? 'Cause your muthafucking ass won't take the time to hit the right spots! But you can take the time to serenade these bitches out here. What about me? Some men don't understand. Won't take the time to explore a woman's body. What is the fuckin' rush, huh? A woman needs patience and understanding, caressing, and arousal. Reaching her climaxing peak takes time and skill, baby. Sometimes a woman wants to rain all over her man, you know what I'm saying? Why deprive her of rain? I don't understand the selfishness. But I will say this: I'm done with your half-assed-dick. What I feel is no

42

different than being constipated. And if you have ever been constipated you know how that feels. Uncomfortable. Bloated. Backed-up. Well, Whupp, I feel all of thee above. The only difference is I'm backed-up with rain. All I want to do is cry. I might as well put an ad in the New York Times to see if there is anyone in the Tri-state area who can make my pussy cry 'cause you men in New Jersey don't seem to know the forecast and I am damn tired of carrying around my umbrella and there ain't no fuckin' rain. Do you hear me, Whupp? Where is the muthafuckin' rain?!!!!

DONE DEAL

September 9, 2008

I can't believe I am steppin' out of Mid State Correctional Facility in Wrightstown, New Jersey, and am on my way back to Bohemia, New Jersey. I can't believe it's been two years. Man, it feels good to be free.

***

The Kid...

As a young man growing up in the Bronx I saw and had experienced many things. I was always the well-dressed and well-spoken young man (I gotta give praise to my moms for those qualities), but livin' in the Bronx you had to have a lil' thug in your blood.

As I think back all I remember was those Timberlands and my swagger as I walked out the door. I thought it was all a dream: manhood, money, and women. Damn, those were the methods to my madness.

In the early days after my father left I saw my mom struggling to raise her son—me. I was only ten when I started thinking of what I could do to get paid. I remember livin' in Manhattan, with my Grandma Rosalind, and my mom. Um, when I think back I was

43

going to public school on Madison Ave and 101st Street. As I was attending school, my mom was attending nursing school, but because of our financial situation and Grandma Rosalind telling her she had to raise her son herself, she never got to fulfill her dream.

Justa give you a little history, my mom was Puerto Rican and my father was African-American. I have a brother and a sister, which I'm the oldest.

Thinking back, basketball usedta be my outlet from my problems at home, but it wasn't enough of an outlet so the streets became my second home. And the rest is…

***

I'm fifteen and the world is looking rather different to me. Like I said, I was the oldest child in my family and I felt like I was the man of the house. Yeah, mom was doing her best to hold things down for us. She landed a job at the Board of Education of New York, even with this job she couldn't give me all the things I desired.

The older guys in the 'hood all seemed to be getting paid. They all drove new cars, and wore the best clothes, and they had fat pockets. This was getting my attention. I was wondering where they were getting this money. Mom kept reminding me that *school* was the most important thing for me to worry about. Because of this I had an 85% grade average in all of my grades. Even though I was doin' my best in school everything around me was really starting to distract me…like girls. Yeah, a brotha had his eye on the coochie. I wasn't ego-trippin' the ladies had their eye on the *kid*.

Now, while on the subject of the coochie let's start by sayin' I was very popular in school, I.S 162 on 149th Street and St. Ann's Ave in the Bronx (intermediate for all you non-educated peoples), just kidding. I attended this school and I graduated from public school in Manhattan. I spent the seventh and eight grades in 162. Brotha' was locking it down with the ladies. Yeah, I had two girlfriends and a coupla of "jump-offs" during my two years in junior high.

My first taste of "pussy" was in the seventh grade. Damn. As I think back, my first piece was Tamika. Tamika Perrez…man, Tamika was half white and half Puerto Rican. She was a sweetheart. We both played in the school band together. She played the flute. I played the trombone. Yeah Tamika was the bessssssstttt flute player in the band. Boy, could she play the flute. That lil' lady could *blow*.

Tamika could play her instrument well, but she could blow me better. It took a little work to get her attention, but when I did it wassa wrap.

We started dating four months into the seventh grade school year. At that time she was my junior high school sweetheart and I thought we would be together for a long time. Tamika and I spent a lot of time together going to the movies and doing homework. We both were very intelligent. That's what I liked about her. She was smart. At first we would just kiss, but the more time we spent together our physical attraction and contact got more and more involved. We began to cut class together. Her mom didn't approve of her having a boyfriend(s). I was Tamika's secret lover. (I gotta chuckle offa that).

My mom would be at work all day. Soooooo we would leave school at lunchtime and go to my house. The first coupla times we were alone we would kiss and she would give me *head*. That was a "tremor" experience. I felt like I was gonna bust that shit in her mouth. Damn! Woo, Tamika was a fuckin' pro at that shit, even though she was a fifteen-year old chick. I mean she would grab my shit and stroke my shit and damn, I had chills go up my spine. Then she would put my dick in her mouth and WOW!!!!!!!! She had me wide open.

Tamika started to fall in love wit' a brotha'. She told me she was getting attached to me, but she was worried her mom would find out about us. Nevertheless, we continued to see each other. I liked Tee a lot, but love. (Pausing) Keepin' it real…nah.

***

Ever since I can remember as a teen I had this certain…how can I put it without sounding "stuck-on-myself" ah, *gift* that would make the females want to be around me or involved with me. Sometimes I think being bilingual with the ability to speak two languages: Spanish and 'Hood had its advantages with the ladies and the fact that I was a "jentleman" gave me the total package.

***

Fall turned into winter and it was getting cold. When I wasn't chillin' wit' Tamika I was at the gym playing basketball. Playing ball was one of the things I enjoyed in life. It took the edge off from the realities of "real" life.

My lil' shorty Tamika would always be sitting on the side of the gym where I was practicing during rec time at school and watch me play. Aiight. Keepin' it real, again. Lil' shorty was keepin' a watch on her dick.

Yeah, I had her but obviously she wasn't sure if she had me. I mean she was there for a reason: to watch the other girls watch me.

Picture this, aiight.

It's February. The week of Valentine's Day, and it's colder than a motherfucker. When I awoke that morning I felt like today was going to be a great day.

Aiight.

When I got to school Tamika was waiting for me outside of my homeroom class. She had on a red crewneck sweater and these tight jeans that hugged her hips. She gave me a hug and passed me a note. She whispered in my ear,

"Let me know at second period class if the answer is yes."

I said. "Okay."

Tamika walked away to her class. I walked in mine and had sat down and began to read.

Hi Baby,

I want to know if we can go to your house today. There is a special day coming up and I don't know if I'm going to see you on the 14th. My mom is sweatin' me. She wants to know my every move. Lemme know at second period Music class, ok.

Love
T.....

I sat for a moment and was alone wit' my thoughts until my homeroom teacher Mrs. Katz interrupted my pleasant state of mind.

Well me being the "jentleman" that I am, I could not deny a young lady her wishes.

Tamika and I left school early. We held hands and hugged and walked to my house. When we got there I put some music on from the little boom box in my room. We began to kiss and touch. I noticed today was different from other days we'd spent together. Tamika was really aggressive and excited.

I began to put my hand in her pants. She didn't stop me. I was surprised.

I opened her pants and started to play with her sweet spot. She reacted to my touching her by grabbing my manhood and massaging me seductively. Her spot was wet with her juices. Damn! She was ready, but she was a little tense.

Aiight.

Brotha gotta admit that I was a little nervous too. But I felt like I was in control. We lay on my bed and continued to touch until she started to take off my clothes. Then I knew it was on and poppin'.

Okay, we were both undressed and got under the sheets. I reached for the nightstand next to the bed and grabbed a condom. I put my jimmy on and sucked on her breasts. She had some pretty pink nipples. I had a thing for breasts. I licked and teased her. Tamika begged me to insert my manhood inside of her. She was sooooooo wet.

I put her legs up and began to enter her love hole. She stopped me for a minute and said, "Please be gentle? You are the first guy I've had sex with."

"Don't worry, baby I won't hurt you."

Tamika and I had sex all afternoon....

This was the beginning of making memories with females. Tamika was the first of many to come. I'll never forget her. The school year was quickly coming to and end. Tee's mom decided they were going to move Down South. After the school year ended Tamika was sad because she didn't want to leave New York. She told me she loved me, but she had to go. When the school year ended we said our goodbyes and went our separates ways.

At this time in my life I didn't know what *love* was. One thing I did know was that I liked the way a girl felt. When I had sex with her, being a jentleman came easy for me, but now I added a new dimension to my personality. I called it the "Player Status"!!!!

***

It's summertime in the 'hood. School was out and everybody on my block was looking to have fun and enjoy the summer break.

My mom was working hard to care for us and keep a roof over our heads. During the summer I had to watch over my brother and sister while my mom worked. 'Round this time my mom started to date this dude named John. He kinda became my step-dad. We didn't get along!!

John was my lil' sister's dad. I had a lil' respect for him but not too much. I went along with the program (not that I had any say anyway) but I felt like I did because that was *my* mom. Aiight. He helped her wit' the bills, but I still felt I could do better than he could.

My brother (Nijel) and I were pretty tight. We usedta chill together and do big bro, lil bro things. Nijel was two years younger than me. As we got older, we started to drift apart. Why? We both took different paths in life, but I still loved him to death. I would give my life for him.

As for my sister (Darlene) our relationship was special. Darlene was mentally handicapped so we really couldn't hold a conversation, but it didn't matter much because "we" knew we were brother and sister. Darlene could not speak because of her condition, but I usedta tell her everyday that I loved her, and I knew she loved me too by the emotion she would show the whole family and me. Taking care of Darlene was a heavy responsibility. I had to step-up to the plate and really become the "man" of the house. My mom was only able to afford part-time care for Darlene. The rest of the time we took care of her ourselves. As soon as Darlene was able to go to a special school, I made sure every morning she got on the school bus, and then I would head to school myself. Being the oldest child in the family wasn't easy. I handled it pretty well, though. I made sure I was there for my family as much as I could be.

Ever since I was a youngster I always had a certain obsession with fashion. I had to have the best sneakers, boots, and the finest clothes…yeah; I had to have it all. Sometimes I think I got it from my dad. Yeah, I based that on the fact that dude was always fresh to def. Mom tried her best to dress me in the same fly shit, but she always was financially limited. So that meant I had to settle for whatever she thought was cool.

In due time I would find a way to get the finer things in life, believe that fly shit. Brother had a plan. You see, because of my demeanor that helped my reputation as being a "jentleman". Yeah, a jentleman for the entire world to see.

***

1983

Summer. I was introduced to the game of hustlin' drugs. There were a few dudes in my 'hood that I considered friends, but for the most part I considered most of them as associates. As far as I was concerned a friend was someone who was real. When I was growing up many dudes didn't qualify as being real.

Two guys I usedta chill wit' were Gene and Mike. They were my teenage running partners. We usedta chase the girls; play sports, things like that. We went to the same school. Yeah, we usedta have a lot of fun.

There was one dude I considered a "real dude". His name was Curl aka C-Money was short, dark-skinned like Wesley Snipes dark. He sported a short clean-cut Afro with his Gucci or Prada gear and Nike sneakers. This dude put me on to the drug game.

My friendship with Curl was different from the one I had with Gene and Mike. It was more of a business relationship between C-Money and me. Don't get it twisted we had a lot of good times while we were gettin' that cash.

C-Money had a brother named Syncere. Syncere was short with this crazy "ditty-bop walk". He was dark-skinned with a clean-cut low-cut fade. He killed gator shoes with slacks and silk shirts. On his layoff days he would sport a velour sweat suit and his Gucci sneakers. Syncere was a big time hustler in the Bronx and in Harlem. Syncere was somewhat of a mystery man. I say that because as I was growing up on the block, before C-Money and me became friends I usedta see Syncere 'round the 'hood. He would come around once and a while. He usedta visit his bro and be out. Syncere was always in a different shiny new ride. He usedta always dress fresh to def. I liked his style. Syncere had this one car. Man, this ride was hot! It was a cranberry red Mercedes Benz with tan interior. Every time I saw him cruise through the 'hood in that whip I said to myself: One day I'm going to have a ride just like that...

One day C-Money and I were in the park playing basketball. While we were waiting for our game to begin I asked C-Money, "What's good with you and my dude?" His response to me was, "Just chillin' Lil' Bro." I said, "I see you doing your thing gettin' that cash. I would like to know if you could put a brother on to the game. My family struggling and I want to help my mom's out." C-Money said, "Hollah at me in a coupla days." My response, "No doubt."

C-Money had the "weed" hustle on lockdown. I figured selling weed should be the easiest hustle I could get involved in since I was so young. So I waited patiently for the day I would get my time to shine.

In the meantime, the summer was going by so quickly. Soon it would be time to go back to school. It's been almost a month now since Tee and me broke up. There were a few females in the 'hood I had my eye on but there was this one girl that really caught my attention. She was a little older than me. This I knew because I asked my boy Gene about her. Gene told me she was already in high school. She was fine as hell. A lot of cats tried to talk to her but should wouldn't give them no play. I didn't know then, but she would be a very special person in my life later on down the line.

I spent the rest of the summer playing in basketball tournaments in the Bronx and in Harlem. When I wasn't ballin' I was watching after my lil' bro and sis. Besides that, I was hanging out with Gene and Mike.

One day my mom asked me to go to the bodega to buy her a gallon of milk. On my way to the store I saw C-Money and his bro Syncere standing on the corner talking. As I approached the corner, C-Money called "Yo, Done c'mere a minute." I stopped to talk to 'em. C-Money said, "Yo, Syn, this is my lil' man Done. He's the one I was tellin' you 'bout."

Aiight.

I'm thinking. Damn, I'm standing on the corner talking to the two big Willie Dudes from my block. I'm feelin' like one of the older cats on the block. Nobody on the block got swagger like these two brothers and I wanted to be like 'em with unlimited swagger.

"What up lil' man?"

"What up, Syncere?"

Syncere leaned his back on the traffic light pole as he swiped a piece of lint of his sky-blue silk shirt and said. "My bro tells me you need a job."

I nodded my head up and down. "Yeah. I need to make some cash."

Syncere remained quiet, looked me dead in my face like he was looking through me and then said, "You'a cool young bro, not like the rest of these knuckleheads out here. I think me and my bro could teach you a few things."

I was eager to express my gratitude. "Yo, Syncere. Man, thanks for giving me a chance. I won't let you down." C-Money kneeled down to wipe the smidgen of dirt off of his fresh white Nike's and then stood putting one hand in his velour sweat suit pants pocket.

"Done, when you get a chance hollah at me so we can talk business."
I gave C-Money and Syncere five and said, "Peace y'all."

As I walked away to head to the store to get the milk for mom I
thought to myself: It's official. I'm in the game. I was happy and
nervous all at the same time. It was a crazy feelin' I had never
experienced before.

Later on I would learn that this feelin' was the feelin' of a "drug-
dealer" feels when he's 'bout to make enough money to change his
life forever! Or so I thought.

The rest of the summer I spent it getting paid. C-Money and me
put a plan together. He would supply me with the drugs and I would
sell them to all the people on my block and in the 'hood.

In two weeks time everybody knew "Lil' Deal" was the man to
see if they wanted weed. I tried my best to hide the fact that I was
getting paid from my mom by letting C-Money hold my profits in his
house. That's one thing about C-Money I was able to trust him. C-
Money taught me the game on another level too. He took me to the
bank and showed me how to hold money in a safe deposit box. He
was like the big brother I never had.

By the time the summer was over I had stacked almost $2500.00.
That was the most money I had ever had in my life. I bought a
couple of outfits for school and two pairs of sneakers. I had to sneak
the clothes and sneakers into my house without my mom noticing. I
got away with keeping my hustle on the down low, but I knew
eventually my mom would find out. That didn't take place for a little
while longer.

***

When I returned to school that next year it was my senior year in
JHS (junior high school). The eighth grade was very interesting to
me. The swagger I had was different. The clothes I wore were better
and I didn't feel like a poor teenager anymore. I had money in my
pocket all the time. I was helping my mom put food on the table. I
was helping with the bills. It felt good to help my family.

I was real busy these days. I was going to school during the day.
After school I would look after my bro and sis until mom got home
from work. Then I would hit the streets to get that cash. C-Money
and I had a schedule. I would work: Monday, Wednesday, Friday,
and Saturday, and sometimes Sunday. I made sure I had time to
study and do my homework on my days off. Man, it's crazy how I
think back now and I laugh about how I usedta call "selling drugs" a

job. I guess that was a way for me to be in an older state of mind. At that time I didn't realize that "selling drugs" was a negative way to earn a living. The way I saw it, I wasn't killing nobody and I wasn't stealing from anyone either so it couldn't be that bad. Later in life I would realize that there were serious ramifications that came with the business of selling drugs.

C-Money had a lot of badass chicks. They were all older than me, but that didn't matter to me. I would throw the "jentleman thug charm" at 'em every chance I got. C-Money always usedta tell me. "You got real game when it comes to the females Lil' Bro." C-Money had one female he was serious about. He usedta call her Wifey. I remember C-Money saying, "Yo, Done, if you ever want to kick it with my other chicks (other than Wifey) that's cool wit' me." I said, "Nah, man, I would never dis you like that. I would never kick it to Wifey, but the other chicks I would do my best to get in da panties."

I was growing up fast hangin' out with C-Money. Being connected with C-Money I was around older people all the time. I was maturing. I believe that's why my maturity level was higher than most dudes my age. C-Money and I would eat at the best restaurants and shop at the best stores like: Macy's and Banana Republic. I was learning how to live life to its fullest.

One night C-Money asked me if I wanted to go out and have a good time with these two honeys. I said, "Hell, yeah!" C-Money had this chick named Diamond Stud. Diamond had a sister name Denise. I had never met Denise before, but if she looked anything like Diamond. Wow!

Diamond was a dark chocolate dime piece. She had a fat ass, pretty face, and a sweet personality. That night we went out to eat dinner at Red Lobster. I was dressed fresh to def. I had on my new Jordan's and a Calvin Klein denim outfit. C-Money had on his Gucci denim suit with the Gucci shoes to match.

It was Saturday night and I was about to go on my first date with an older female. We got into C-Money's black and gold Audi. Diamond and Denise lived across town from us. C-Money drove while, I sat back enjoying the music. Eric-Band Rakim was pumpin' out of C-Money's speakers. We picked up the beautiful ladies around 8:00 p.m. We pulled up in front of their house. The niggas on their block was sweatin' us. They looked like they were wondering who are these two big ballers. C-Money got out the car and said, "What up?" to one tall, young buck whom C-Money put on. C-Money had jokers pushin' weed on Diamond's block too. *Damn, this nigga is gettin' paid*, I thought.

When C-Money finished talking to the dude, the same dude walked over to the car and gave me a paper bag. The young buck said, "C-Money said hold on to this." By then C-Money had walked inside the corner store to get some cigarettes. When I opened the bag there was like one thousand dollars in it. C-Money returned back to the car and got in. "Did my boy give you that bread?" I said, "Yeah." He said, "Put that in your pocket. I want you to pay for whatever tonight. I want you to feel like you're the man tonight." I said, "Good lookin' out, Curl." He said, "Anytime Lil' Bro. That chick Denise is really going to be sweatin' you tonight, Lil' Bro. You might just fuck her tonight you know what I mean." I gave him five and we both started laughing. The night had just started and already I was having fun.

Just about then, Diamond and Denise came out of the house. When I saw Denise I said, "Damn! C-Money that chick looks good as hell!" C-Money cut his eye over at me and said, "You know I only associate with dime pieces." I got out of the car and opened the back door for Denise. She got in and Diamond sat in the front with C-Money, while I sat in the back with Denise. We got to Red Lobster. C-Money had made reservations so we didn't have to wait for a table. While we waited for dinner C-Money ordered drinks (I was only 16 so I couldn't order alcohol.) The waitress brought over the drinks. C-Money and the females drank rum and Coke while I had a regular Coke.

Our dinner arrived and we got our eats on. It was the first time I had lobster and shrimp. (This would become my favorite dish.) After dinner, the ladies wanted to drink a little bit more. C-Money said, "Ok." I asked for the check and paid for dinner and then we moved over to the bar. C-Money and the ladies sipped on their drinks and I sipped on my soda. Denise and I were having a great time. My conversation with her was going good. At one point she asked me if I wanted a little bit of her drink. I said, "Yeah." So she gave me some. Denise was feelin' a little tipsy. Yeah, I could tell. I was feelin' a little tipsy too. She started grabbing my hand and I started to feel like she wanted the kid to give her the magic stick. The girls ordered one more drink, but this time Denise ordered a pina colada for me. The drink had rum in it so I was feelin' niccccccccccccceee.

Denise was really enjoying how I was talking to her. She spoke in a sweet child-like voice and said, "For a young man you a real charmer." I said, "Thank you. By the way, how old are you?" She giggled and said, "I'm twenty-six. Why do you ask?" I said, "Just curious. You're a fine woman." She glued those bedroom eyes on me and said, "Thank you, Done."

Denise was five feet five inches of thick light skin. She had the fattest ass and nice titties. She looked a little like Mary J. Blige.

The ladies went to the rest room, while they were gone C-Money said, "Yo, Done, Denise and Diamond want to go to a hotel. Diamond told me Denise is really feelin' your swagger." I was all hyped up. "Let's go, C!" C-Money said, "Aiight. When they come back we're going to tell 'em we're out of here." I paid the bill for the drinks. Two minutes later the ladies returned.

We left the restaurant and headed to the Ramada Hotel. On the ride to the hotel Denise and I were kissing and touching one another in the backseat. Denise kept grabbing my dick like she wanted me to fuck her right then and there. In my mind, I was thinking I'm going to bust this fine honey's ass tonight. When we got to the lobby C-Money went to the desk and got two keys. He paid for the room with his credit card. He handed one key to me and said "See you in the morning." I took the key and Denise and I headed up to our room.

When we got in the room I turned on the stereo. There were slow jams playing on the radio. Denise started to get undress. She looked at me and said, "I'm going to take a quick shower. Do you want to join me?" I did not hesitate in responding. "Sure." Denise walked into the bathroom and started the shower while I got undress. There was a Jacuzzi in the room. I turned it on and the bubbles started to flow. I got in the shower with Denise. I looked at her. She had a gorgeous body. There was soap all over her. She lathered the soap and started to lather my body down. While she was doing that she grabbed my dick and started to stroke it back and forth. I began to play with her sweet spot. She was getting mad horny. Soon we both were hot and bothered. We rinsed the soap off of ourselves and I started to suck on her big tits. She was going crazy while I sucked her nipples.

Denise got down on her knees and started to suck my dick. Wow! I had never fucked a female in the shower before (I thought to myself: tonight I'm making another memory.) Denise stopped sucking my dick and stood up and turned around. She bent that pretty ass over and said in the softest seductive tone I'd ever heard, "Done, fuck me, please. Fuck me." so the kid obliged. I grabbed her by her hips and entered her pussy from behind. She moaned loudly. While stroking her pussy I said, "Denise, your pussy feels so goooooooood." I pounded her for about fifteen minutes. Then we stopped and got out of the shower and went straight to the Jacuzzi. We got in the water. The sensation of the water made me very excited. My cock got hard, again. Denise began to ride my dick like she was riding a horse. Eventually we got out of the Jacuzzi and lay in the bed. We talked, not long, though. I turned on the TV, and put on the porn channel. Soon we were fucking again. I had her on all fours hitting it from the back. Bang, bang, bang!!!!

Denise looked good with her ass in the air. I was really enjoying this older pussy. While I was fucking her good, Denise said, "Wow! For a young nigga you fuck like a grown man. The Lord done blessed you with a big tool." That boosted my ego reallll quick. Soon I pulled my dick out and exploded all over her fat ass. I think we fucked for like four hours (on and off) that night.

I got home around 8 o'clock that morning. My mom asked me where I was all night and I recall saying, "I was with this girl I met at the party last night." My mom said, "Boy, don't be making no babies out there! You too young to be a father." I said, "Don't worry, mom, I won't make you a grandma anytime soon." She said, "You betta' not!"

***

Funny-style nigga

My senior year was going by quickly. Even though I was busy in the streets I made sure my grades didn't suffer. That made my mom happy. She was excited that I was going to graduate to high school this year. Even though I felt like things were going great at this point and time in my life—everything wasn't good. My mom and her "funny-style-nigga" John were having problems. They were always arguing. That shit had me stressed out. I didn't like the fact that he would be yelling at her.

One night they had a big fight. I wasn't home. But when I got home my mom was in the bathroom crying. She had her face in her hands. I said, "Mom, what happened?" she didn't want to answer me. I asked her again. Then I put two and two together. I said, "You and that nigga had a fight!" Then she looked at me. Her left eye was bruised. John had *slapped* her. My eyes widened, drooped, and then darkened. I wanted to kill that bitch-ass nigga. I had to try to calm myself down but it was mad hard. "Mom, if he ever comes back to this house I'm going to hurt him reallllll bad." I was not kidding. Mom nervously swayed her head as her eyes flooded into bigger tears that streamed down her weary face. "Done, no, please, no. Please don't do anything crazy," she spoke in a trembling voice. I could see the fear outlined in her eyes and that pissed me off even more.

Sometime after that situation with John, mom didn't see him again. Yeah, it was a done deal for real. I considered that bitch-ass nigga lucky, not blessed. Lucky.

***

There was this girl at school. She was fine as hell! Her name was Vanessa. Vanessa was in the seventh grade. She was Puerto Rican. This female wassa dime piece. She looked older than fifteen. Her body was built like an eighteen-year-old chick. She was very pretty. She had a bubble of an ass and she could dress real fly. When I first noticed her I tried to kick-it to her, but she wouldn't give me the time of day. She was reallll conceited, but there was one thing about me I was very persistent. If I worked hard enough, I got what I wanted.

One day I was at my locker in the school hallway, when Vanessa walked by. I said, "What up, Vanessa?" She said, "Hi, Done, how you doing?" I said, "I'm just chillin'. You lookin' realll cute, today." She said, "Thank you." Then I said, "Yo, Vanessa, why don't you want to talk to me?" Vanessa stood still and said, "Well, I heard you have a lot of girls chasin' you." I didn't deny it. "Yeah, I got a lotta female friends, but there's no one special right now." I asked her for her phone number and she gave it to me. Before she walked away she said, "Call me tonight and we can talk some more." I smirked and said, "Aiight. Cool."

That night Vanessa and I stayed on the phone until 1:00 a.m. We talked about a lot of things but we spoke mostly about her being my girlfriend. She said that she would think about it. I knew she would come around. I mean who could resist me. I wassa handsome, articulate, charming muthafucker with a big dick.

Soon Vanessa and I were taking long walks in the park. She would come over to my house and I would go over to hers. I took her to the movies a few times. We mostly kissed nothing too crazy. That was okay with me because we were getting to know each other. We were seeing each other for about three months.

One day I was in the schoolyard around lunchtime and this short dude with dark hair and mango-colored skin approached me. He said, "Yo Done, my boy Derek wants to talk to you for a minute." so I walked over to see what this Derek joker wanted. When I got over to Derek I said, "What up?"

Lemme give you some quick info about this joker Derek. First of all he's an older dude. You know one of those high school aged nigga's that like to hang out around the JHS so he could talk to the young girls. Derek was like eighteen or nineteen years old. I really didn't know him personally, but I knew what he was about because I usedta see him around the school all the time. He didn't know me that well, but he knew I sold weed in the 'hood because his boys usedta buy their weed from me. He lived on the other side of the park in the J-Projects. There was a big park in my 'hood called St. Mary's Park. It separated one 'hood from the other because it was so big. In the summer I usedta play ball there all the time.

Derek stood lookin' tough and shit. "Yo, I heard you talking to my girl."

"What girl you talking about?" I said with a puzzled look upon my face.

"You know, nigga. You know who da fuck I'm talking about. Her name is Vanessa."

Now, I'm thinking to myself: This is news to me. So I said, "Look my brother, I've been seeing Vanessa for like three months and she ain't mention nothing to me about having a boyfriend."

Derek stared me in my face like I was 'sposed to shake in my joints and shit. "Well, I'm here to let you know stay away from her or you're going to have a problem with me."

I smirked. This nigga threatening me. "Look, I don't care who da fuck you are or how old you is you might have some of these other punk-ass nigga's scared of you, but I ain't one of 'em."

Mind you the whole time he's talking to me he had his hand in his pants pocket and four of his boys were standing with him. The only person I had with me was my friend Mike.

"So you think you'a gangster because you sell a little weed lil' nigga."

At that moment Derek pulled a .22 caliber from his pants pocket. I stepped back. I kinda froze seeing my life flash before my eyes and shit. But I wasn't going to punk out and let this nigga chump me.

"Nigga you better shoot me now, because if you don't you ain't going to be able to sleep at night because I'm coming to get your punk-ass."

As soon as I said those words he struck me on the head striking me on top of my right eye. When he swung to hit me I closed my eyes because I thought he was going to shoot me, but I didn't hear the gun go off. I felt the cold steel hit me and blood started to drip down my face. Derek ran off and so did his little bitches. My boy Mike said, "Done, you alright?" I felt dizzy from the blow. I had to stand still for what seemed like a minute or two just to regain myself. Then I said in a faint voice, "I think so." I didn't go back to school. I went straight home.

When I got to my block my friends had asked me what happened. I told 'em. They told me don't worry we gonna take care of this shit for you. So I did as I was told. I didn't worry 'bout shit. I went home and cleaned myself up. I notice I only had a small cut so I was able to hide it from my mom. If she did notice I had my plan set to tell her it happened while I was playing basketball.

When mom came home from work I acted like nothing happened. I tried to call Vanessa, but I couldn't get in contact with her for some unknown reason. C-Money wasn't around that week because him and Syncere had to go out of town to handle some business.

Later that day my boys came to my house to tell me that they were going to shoot up J-Projects where Derek lived. They told me that they didn't need me to go with 'em. That they were going to handle it themselves.

Later on that night my boys went over to Derek's 'hood and bust their guns. I could hear the gunshots from my room window. I was nervous because if my boys killed Derek I knew it would come back on me because people at school saw what had happened.

Finally Vanessa called me after school let out. She was crying. I said, "What's up?" Vanessa said, "Sorry. I heard what happened to you at school. Um, Derek came to my house and told me that somebody shot up his projects."

I asked her, "You seeing Derek?"

"He is only a friend. We can talk tomorrow at school."

"Okay." I said, and hung up the phone.

The next morning, I went to school. I saw my boy Mike.

"Yo, Done, I was there with the rest of my boys. We shot up the projects, but no one got hurt. They just wanted that joker Derek to know that he can't fuck with anybody from our 'hood, especially C-Money's boy."

I nodded my head up and down and said, "Good lookin' my nigga. Good lookin'."

DONE I TWAT

September '08-City Welfare

As I've said I've since retired, but I used to be a caseworker for the Board of Social Services on Tabor Street, downtown Bohemia, and handling clients applying for City Welfare. I remember like it was yesterday. This *young* gentleman named Done Deal was sitting among the others who were waiting to be called. Faces of minorities, young and old were scattered in the orange and blue seats. Of course, not all were there applying for City Welfare. Some were already receiving their benefits. Others were there to get passes to go to Service to see if they could get assistance for their PSE&G bills, vouchers, etcetera. There was a thick, clear partition separating the clients from the workers just in case someone got stupid and started threatening to do harm to someone because they didn't receive their check, food stamps, or Medicaid card. Working for the State was definitely unpredictable. People would blackout over money they felt they had worked a forty-hour week and earned.

I stepped in room 008, and of course all eyes were on me.

"Done Deal." I called out with confidence in my voice and I might add a fresh, crisp J. Crew charcoal gray pants suit complemented by a soft baby blue ribbed turtleneck accentuated by my chocolate brown Charles David T-strap heels. And my makeup was flawless. I had a glow as if I had just had multiple orgasms. Yes, that kinda glow.

My eyes scanned the room and then this nice looking, tall, young man, (*young* being the operative word), rose to his feet with swagger in his step. Hands in his jacket pocket, snug hat on his head, and eyes that could've saw right through me. My first impression of him was *delicious*.

"Follow me." I said with a little switch in my voluptuous hips.

Done eyes were glued to me. We stepped into my office, which really was a small cubical.

"Have a seat."

Done sat down, his eyes wandered a little admiring the pictures displayed on my desk, and then he planted those bad boys back on me. My body was growing hot, but not bothered.

I grabbed a red folder and wrote his name at the top as I'd asked. "Do you have your birth certificate and ID?"

"Yeah." he said, while pulling some papers out of his jacket pocket. Then, he placed them on the desk.

"Have you tried to collect unemployment?"

"I haven't worked."

Then he generously advised me that he was recently released from prison.

There is no reason for me to ask the next question: Did he vote because I know that he can't with a felony record. Not to stereotype but I kinda had a feeling he just got of prison based on his muscular physique. It was either that or he enjoyed working out. I was glad he volunteered the information.

"How are you supporting yourself?" I asked.

"I'm staying with a relative."

"I'm going to need a letter from that relative."

"I got it."

My eyes cut to the side. "You have it?"

"Yeah. I kinda figured you'd need some type of document."

Hmm. I like that. He is on his job. There is something about him that piques my interests.

He pulled the letter out of his inside pocket of his jacket and laid it on my desk. My eyes scanned it quickly.

"Um, you may want to write." I paused and glanced at the handwriting of the letter and the cursive signature. "Is this your handwriting?"

"Yeah. I wrote the letter and my aunt signed it."

"Do you have the same pen on you?"

"Yeah."

"Okay. Just write underneath that you have to supply your own food."

He reached for the letter as I noticed his hands were quite ashy, but those eyes. *Mmm.*

While I was printing out the paperwork I explained his benefits.

"Mr. Deal, normally I'll have thirty days to complete your file but usually I have it done before the deadline. You'll be entitled to one hundred and forty dollars. You're food stamps will be one hundred and seventy-six. And Medicaid. Once my case manager signs off on this you'll receive a letter to come back and see me." I smiled. "Here is my card should you have any questions before that time. I just need your signature on these forms." He reached for *my* pen. I felt the tips of his fingers they were hot. While he was signing I went over the don'ts of his benefits.

"Mr. Deal, please don't give false information or hide any information. Don't trade or sell your Family First Card. Don't allow someone else's family to use your card. And, please, don't use food stamps to buy alcohol or tobacco. If you do any of these things your benefits will be terminated."

As Done signed he nodded his head indicating he understood. While he signed the several pieces of paper I stood and walked to the copier to make a copy of his birth certificate and ID.

I returned and sat down. I tapped the papers on my desk to even them out. Then, I signed where needed and stuffed them in his file and plop it on top of the others piled on my desk.

"Thanks." He said, as he stood and tucked the business card in his back pants pocket and walked out of my cubical.

I really couldn't get an eyeful of his ass because his pants were too saggy. Shit.

Most of the men I met were from work. Work had every kind of man there: thug, hustler, psycho, and wino, intellectual, mental case. You name it City Welfare had its share. So I really didn't have to look very far. There were so many men getting out of prison, in rehab, or a shelter. Like I said there were more men that I cared to count. But when I laid eyes on Done like I said it was something different about him. What? I didn't know but knowing me I was bound to find out.

Now, of course, there was a line that could not be crossed because that would be considered fraternizing with a client. So I had to be discreet as possible. I managed to only see Done off-hours, mostly on the weekends. That was my time and what I did on my time was my goddamn business.

I met Twat. I wanted Twat. Who wouldn't with her fine ass? There is nothing more attractive than a fine ass older woman. I questioned whether or not I could get her. I didn't know, but with the charm that I displayed there was a good chance at best. And as it did happen the chance presented itself. Call it luck, charm, or fuckin' gift of gab. It really didn't matter to me as long as I hit the skins.

Twat had a certain sensuality about her. It didn't jump out at you. No. But it was deep in her soul. I saw it when I looked deep into her eyes. I wanted to get closer, more personal. I guess the timing wasn't right back in 2008 because she was involved with someone. Who knew a year later, 2009, we would bump into each other again at the Dirty-Mouth Sports bar on Bolton (crossed streets of Medford and Oxford) across from the 24-hour Tick-Tock.

***

152 Cianci Ave

It is a stab in the dark but I invite Twat to my house. That's how the shit jumped off. I have a room: a bed, a cabinet, a TV, a chair, and one window. I have to share the bathroom with the other tenants—all men. All Hispanic. Knowing this, Twat comes along anyways. I know then that she isn't the gold-digger type. She is sexy, slim, and smart. Having her in the presence of my home makes me feel privileged. I am yearning for some TLC. I guess the aphrodisiac is this November rain. Yeah, I said *rain.*

The spring-shower smell cascades through the screen of the window. The sound is like soft melody of Maxwell. It definitely sets the mood. We sit and eat take-out dinner. Talk about many things. She gets comfortable by taking her shoes off, and lay across my bed. Looks into my eyes. Smell my scent of "safe" and "original." I ask her to spend the night. I clean the tub out for her to take a hot shower. We sip on 22-ounce Natural Ice (that is all I can afford) and enjoy the evening. And then we fuck. It is amazing. She feels soft. I kiss and caress her. Twat is so seductive. She tells me to lay back and relax. She gets on top of me and straddles my dick. And begins to ride me. Her pussy feels soooo tight. I want to explode, but I hold it back (well, nigga tries…hard). Twat begins to fuck with an up and down motion. Next thing I know she rise above me and sprays me all over my chest with her cum. I have never experienced anything like this before. She is pouring her cum on me like a water fountain. This rain turns me on. And yes, a nigga wants more. I am hooked. But—

Kake. That's my girl. Yeah, that chick had my back. I gotta give it to her. Do I love her? Honestly…um, no. But she is a good woman. She has stuck by my side through thick and thin. I care for her deeply. But we don't spend much time together. Look, it was bad enough being locked the fuck up away from the pussy and now that I am home I can't even get a nibble on the regular. That's some bullshit! I understand family is important to Kake. That's what I like about her. She's a good girl. But *what about me? Where do I fit in?* I won't press the issue with her because we have had this conversation before and I seem to get nowhere. It's been the same since I've been released from prison. But that's in the past. I'm home now. Kake had all these plans while I was incarcerated but once I got home things changed. Everything changed. I guess she was trying to hold a brother down. But I don't need to be held down unless she is on top of me loving me down. I have a high sex drive and Kake is not steering me strong. Nah. I guess she thinks that I'm happy going to bed with a hard-on. Obviously she does because she is not here fucking my brains out. And I am tired of stroking *Amigo*, you feel me? Well, in the midst of these changes with her I bumped into Twat at Bryant Park in New York. It just so happened that she was alone so we spent a little time together soaking up the fall air. From there we decided to see each other. Twat had gave me the scoop on her marriage, but I didn't care because I wanted to get that *pussy*. So my world of loneliness became a world of unbelievable pleasures with this vivacious woman. Yeah, I had my Kake and I was eatin' Twat too. You might as well call the Pound 'cause a dog has just gotten loose.

O-kkkkkkkkaaaaakayyyy. How do I really feel about Done? Safe. Calm. Heard. Appreciated. Liked. He's like a dream come true—too good of a dream. He has that Blair Underwood flair. I like men who can carry a conversation that doesn't sound "street" like a recording of Hip-Hop. He constantly smiles. Kinda sly. His eyes are his best assets to me. They are hypnotizing. His height of six feet is a bonus.

I love a tall man. Let me stop dreaming for a moment and check myself. *Girl, you are dead wrong to be seeing him knowing that he has her.* Okay. I've gotten it off of my chest, but that won't stop me from seeing him. I mean c'mon. Let's be serious here. I finally get to rain and I'm expected to go back to my drought! Fuck thattttt!!!! No! I miss this feeling. Okay. Let's get down to it.

You wanna discuss *her*—his main squeeze. Okay. I'll give her a brownie point for sticking by his side through the good and the bad times. She waited for him to get out of prison for two years. Whoop-de! She has supported him during his up and downtime. And? She isn't here now. Where is she? Working two jobs. Raising two kids. Still, living with her parents and trying to have a fulfilling relationship. I hate to say it but girly is not meeting all of her priorities. What about da dick? Had she forgotten that *it* needs love too? I think so. I should know because while he is on the phone with her I am slopping and sucking and licking his dick and balls buck-naked in his bed that she bought. If she is soooo perfect why am I here? Where is she? Home. Why isn't she tending to her man? Maybe because she feels she has him wrapped around her finger or vice versa. *Trust.* What's that? She thinks or at least he has her convinced that he isn't going anywhere. That life goes on and they are going to be living in bliss. The bitch must be blind because even I could sense that something was missing wayyyyy before I fucked him. He needs his ego stroked—to feel a soft being in his bed—to look at his woman staring him in the face comes morning. Her smile. Her laughter. Energy. Her genuine concern for his well-being. Her ear to listen making him feel significant. Making him feel like a man. I'm here, not her. It takes little to satisfy Done. It takes what I have to give, which is this seasoned twat that cums in eleven different flavors.

LET IT RAIN

277 Liverpool Way

The phone rings.
I turn on my side and answer it. "Hello." I say in a sleepy voice.

All I hear is heavy breathing. "PERVERT stops calling this number whoever you are!" I slam the phone in its cradle and roll back over to go back to sleep.

Five minutes later the phone rings, again.

Damn! Who da hell keeps playing on this phone? "Hello. Hello. HELLOO!"

I hear laughter. "Who da hell is this playing on my damn phone?!" The person keeps on laughing. I am about to hang up when I hear. "Twat, come open the door, baby."

Suddenly I recognize the voice. "Why da hell are you playing on the phone, moron. It's 2:30 a.m., and why are you at my house? Are you crazy? How'd you know I was here alone?"

"Twat, open the door? I'm sorry. Look, I saw my manz leave, earlier. Look, a nigga's fucked up and my joint is hard as hell." That is all I need to hear. I leap out of bed; pull off my panties and rush to open the door. As soon as I open the door, Done has his dick drawn waiting to stick it in my wet pussy.

I open my eyes and stare into Done's eyes of erotica. His lips are moist and full as he glides his salivating tongue against the skin of my navel. His face, forehead, and baldhead are all drenched in sweat. Dripping like rain on a windowpane, sea-salt moisture glistens against my bare skin making me look sexier than ever. Mmm. He is strong and generous with his lust. The balls of my eyes roll as if experiencing convulsions. Oh, the feel of his thick dick caresses my silky wet walls so gently. *Ugh, ugh, ugh*, escapes from me, as his thrusts grow strong, more in rhythmic flow that makes my head bob against the sex-smelled air. The top of my forehead is beading with wetness as his long tongue licks it off, and then pecks my soft full lips. My long legs wrap around his sodden back, feet crisscross as I hold him tightly. *Oh, oh, oh, ugh, ugh ugh ugh*. He inches upward and sucks on my nipples and pulls 'em with his sharp teeth. *Ugh, ugh, ugh*. Then he melts my left tit in his mouth and massages it with his hot, hot, hot spit. Never have I experienced this kind of lust making. It is the kind that will persuade you to melt him in your mouth like a milk chocolate M&M. I am trying to erase the thought from my mind, but the intense feeling he is delivering sweeps across my stomach and shoots down to my pussy taunting it to pleasure this body of magnificence. I feel the urge to swallow, slobber down his pole, twist and curl my tongue around his tool and hide him in the walls of my hot, slimy mouth. Spiraling my glossy tongue around his

65

head and licking the sides of his dick with seduction. Moaning, "Oh, Dickey." Groaning, "Oh, shiiitttttt!" Sucking with that smacking sound, (slop, slop, slop) and swallowing a big gulp of cream down my throat while tickling his pee-hole with the tip of my tongue, forth and back movements, poppin' my lips to tease and taunt him. I want to fuck his head up. I want to let the "rain goddess" Chocolate Twat reappear. Stroke his ego. I pause, just briefly, and stare in his chestnut-brown eyes and I let go.

Inching down to his big-bone dick. Holding it with a cupped fist—hard and vigorously I choke that muthafucker. I spit on the *head* as it dribbles down the sides and I lick it like an ice cream cone. Mmm. Then I peck it for good behavior. Tonguing it lovingly— French kissing it erotically. The tip of my tongue slides across it, down, and back up. I open my mouth wider and devour him feeling his body shudder.

His eyes flutter, his teeth bite down on his bottom lip, hard, almost breaking the skin as he stutters in a whisper, "Twat, you're a fucccccckin' tiger."

He feels my lust. The heat. The flaming fire burning in my loins. And I feel distant eyes of guilt staring at me. And I know it comes from knowing of her—that special someone whose dick I am indulging heavily in. She knows nothing of what is transpiring between *his* sheets. She knows nothing about me. *This could be deadly*, I think. *Yes*, I respond, while riding him. Briefly I think of her. Very briefly, as his massive hands squeeze my ass, and lick the lips of my pussy with his moist finger. She crosses my mind again, as I raise my body slightly, squint, and press my lips together feeling the sensation building inside of me. My head tilts back, while my ass and rotating hips hump him hard. Then I rise up just a little and let nature do its thing. I let it rain. Pouring. Gushing from my sweet and liberating pussy onto his tight stomach. His eyes pierce at it flowing out of me. Then he cracks a sly smile and squeezes my ass, again. I feel exhilarating, as does he. My lust juices flow like a faucet.

"Damn, Twat, that never happened to me before."

Shit, I feel powerful. *Someone will get hurt*, I think. *This is wrong*, I think, again, but I can't resist the temptation of his lust feeding my need. I yearn to rain—to feel sexy and in control. Liberal. Done give me it all. *I have to be careful. Things can really get ugly especially with me being happily married.*

All of a sudden, Done and I hear what sounds like footsteps creeping up the stairs. Done leaps out of bed and grabs his clothes. I leap up running around the room buck-naked trying to figure out what to do before Whupp waltzes in and catches us. I open the window while Done is hurrying to get dress and he climbs out the window, down the maple tree, as I wipe my sweaty forehead and jump back into bed and turn the nightlight off. I hear the door squeak open as I pretend to be asleep, but as I am about to shut my eyes I notice a gold wrapper on the floor near the nightstand. Oh shit, it's an empty Magnum wrapper. All I can think is Whupp don't come any closer and please, please, baby, don't come on my side of the bed to talk, kiss, or anything. *Okay, Twat, how da fuck are you going to get out of this one. It ain't like you can use sex as your ploy because Whupp hasn't fucked you for two years, girl.* Okay, okay. Hopefully he'll go back downstairs to the basement. Hopefully.

"Twat, baby, you'a sleep?"

I ignore him as I hear him walk out of the bedroom and head back downstairs. I leap out of bed and grab the wrapper and run into our master bathroom and flush it down the toilet.

BEAUTIFUCK

Look, my life is no Jack and Jill saga because I don't run after no man. I must admit, though, I have a tendency to do most crimes most women my age won't even think of attempting. But I almost never pay the price of my actions and I certainly pay you no-never-mind in the end. I am too shrewd to have a care in the world. Twat's world consists of no worries, no heartache, and no more pain. I am way beyond those crocodile tear years. There are no harps, violins, or love ballads filtering around me with birds chirping that I'm in love or professing my undying love for my man. Nope. Those days are long gone. This voluptuous woman that I stare at has high standards and deep pockets. I made my goldmine by being intelligent, hard working, and by keeping my eyes and options open. I keep my body tight, toned, and smelling, oh so delicious. And the most important thing you should know is that I am a grown-ass woman. I have retired from hard labor, but I won't retire from stroking men with a hard-on. Call me what you will, but know that life is b-e-a-u-t-i-f-u-l. And beauty deserves to be fucked doggy-style.

I enjoy entertaining. I enjoy my get-a-ways every month-end. And no, I don't pay a dime out of my pocket. Chile, don't make me laugh. Why should I pay when he is getting all of this beautiful pussy wrapped onto his arm? I make him look good. And while doing all of this I still keep my man at home happy. *How*, you may ask. Well, I have an answer by being his loving wife, friend, and confidant. I treat him like the king that he is, and he in turn keeps me sane. Every woman wishes she had what I have. But all of us can't be as fortunate. I've realized the younger we are, the dumber and more delusional we become. That's where we make our biggest mistake believing that man will love us until death do us part. Puuullllleeeeeaaassseeee. As soon as his tired ass gets up from laying down his law, he is off to feed his next kitty while you; Mrs. Gullible is home playing wifey. No. I ain't the one. The bullshit stops here!

Don't get it twisted my husband Whupp is a priceless gem. But sometimes after so many years of marriage feelings tend to change. Marriage becomes a job. And that was where things went wrong with me. I needed fun and excitement in my life. Those golden years had already caught up with me. I needed and wanted to feel young, vivacious, and sexy. Whupp loves me dearly, but somewhere in our thirty years of marriage the flames burnt out between us. We haven't made love in two-years. Two! Work took over our lives and the routine began to dictate our marriage. The debonair man no longer tingled my coochie. The man, who back in the day used to have abs, now has a potbelly. The silky black hair turned silver. The energetic and frisky man just sits in his Harlowe olive-green swivel recliner like an old man. Spontaneity died. And life became generic. I am far from old. I have to keep telling myself that. I don't feel old and I ain't gonna start now. Whupp. Well, that man is set in his ways and I can't do anything about it nor am I trying to. I am content with him being home. That's right. I know the whereabouts of my man.

I recall when I was a naïve adolescent; mama (god bless her soul) shared something deep with me. You see I was once young and delusional at the age of seventeen. Um, this was around the time Whupp and I decided to take a break because things were getting too serious, too soon. I met this young man named Taylor Jefferson. Taylor was gorgeous, tall, dark, and arrogant. He was twenty-three years old, but I lied and told mama he was eighteen. I met him at this pizza shop over on Sole Ave, next to the Laundromat (SUDS WASH-N-DRY) Mama and I frequented every Saturday morning. I was head-over-heels for that man, but Taylor was a dog in heat. I was faithful to him. I loved that man to death. And Taylor loved down every other woman in his bed. I was beyond crushed. God I wanted to die. I loved him so much. The pain was unbearable.

Mama. She told me that with all the men in this world that there was no way in hell one woman could be content with just one dick. I soon discovered that Mama was telling on herself. But I never snitched on her because her boyfriend was boring as hell. She needed some excitement in her life. The more pleasure she got. The more pleasurable and generous she was with me. I remember her words verbatim. She said *if you could have a man for every day of the week then you were the baddest hoe in the city of DeWitt.* Well, Mama wasn't lying. I am as bad as they come. I waited late in life to be a hoe, but better late than never.

There are no hang-ups in my way. I don't take things personal. And I don't have to pretend. The good thing is that I really don't give a damn about much these days. I don't believe I'm gonna say this but thank goodness for menopause! I deal with men much younger because of their stamina. I don't want a man on Viagra. What a waste. I desire men of multiple talents in the bedroom. Who actually sticks to the three-month rule? Scratch that. I know someone all too well, my ex girlfriend V. Yes, I gotta little bi-curious in me. She is on this celibacy journey. Good luck, girl, 'cause I can't do it. I say that to her every time we talk.

By the time I pick up my piece I know if he is going to be my dessert. Usually I get that warm feeling in between my legs. Yeah, I get slippery wet. That is my signal and once I get that I just let the night ride. And by midnight usually I am riding him till the crack of dawn. I'll fuck him so good that by the second, third, and before the fourth fuck he is submissive to me. This is when the list comes out of all the things I desire. Don't get it twisted every man aims to please. Once he is hooked—on to the next. That's right. If I can find a man who can make this here kitty purr I might have to leave my husband for good. Thus far, I haven't met my match. But when I do you best cover your ears 'cause there is gonna be a loud KABOOM!

I'm a big girl and big girls don't cry. Huh. We make our men cry in bed. Forget about calling my name, brother cry...cry me some crocodile tears. That's what I say. When you have that kind of power to do that, you know you are the shits. Listen to me and you won't have any regrets. But if you keep fantasying and daydreaming and screwing every ding that dongs, honey, you will never keep your pretty feet planted on the ground, but you will always keep your legs up in the air with a dickhead b'tween 'em. Now, which do you prefer? Cryme or Punyshment 'cause I know both of those skanky bitches all too well.

STINKY SEX

152 Cianci Ave

The Nextel bleeper bleeps and breaks *our* sleep. We both are lying in our bare skin. I am on the right. And he is on the left side of *his* bed—neither one of us make a move until it bleeps again. Then, Done reaches to answer it. And I roll over on my side, unconcern.

"Hello." he whispers.

I open my eyes and look at the clock on the wall that reads 9:30 a.m. I cover my head with the comforter and try to tune him out. His conversation is brief. Done says his good-byes to *her* and snuggles his hot skin against mine. With bad breath, crust in our eyes, and the residue of last night's sexing we can't resist the heat between our legs.

"I haven't even washed up yet, Done."

He has a lust look in his eyes. I know what he wants without him speaking it but he feels the need to express himself. "I don't care. I want you." Then he speaks that shit in Spanish. I surrender. "Dammit, fuck me bilingual-man!"

His body rises and gets on top of me. He kisses my neck and lips and slides his dick in me so gently that I automatically raise my legs and let him get his breakfast on. Stinky sex is the best sex for us. We are very comfortable with one another. And that just keeps the fire burning between us. I am not worried about Kake, if anything she had better be worried about me. I am giving her part-time lover the best sex he has ever had. And in return, he is giving me time, patience, understanding, and as much dick one pussy can stomach, but somewhere along the way things began to change. I feel a drought coming on. Maybe his mind is preoccupied, I don't know, but he isn't making me feel that storm dying to come pouring down. No. I need stimulation. I need dirty sex talk. I need to feel in control and sometimes he makes me feel powerless. That just takes the oomph away from me and I become ordinary. I hate to be ordinary! I need to be spectacular. Desirable. Phenomenal. Yes, it is quite difficult for Done to make me rain. And that only creates friction between the sheets. I become bored just like with Whupp. He can have his Kake with the icing because I feel the fizz fizzling. I don't care how much of my pussy he eats it does nothing for me. If that tongue can't make me drool it is a waste of time. But Done will not let the pussy go. And truthfully, I am just rambling on. Done is too good of a man to let slip through the cracks. There are some things I can tolerate and him not being able to make me rain is one. He is a rarity in my book. A sweet and charming young buck that knows how to work his dick. I can cum so that isn't an issue. It's just that sometimes my pussy yearns to rain. And since Done has the experience I know that he will try his very best to accommodate me. And if he can't, I guess I'll have to let my middle finger stroke my kitty Koo-Koo until that pussy purrs herself to sleep.

He's fine.
I'm giving up on men!
He's fine.
I'm tired of the bull-crap with men!
He's fine.
That's it. I'm done with men!
He's fine.
I'm through with men!
He's fine.

Damn, girl will you please make up your mind! Kake Mahogany, get a grip. You've got Dick String-A-Long on the brain. I know. You must admit he is fine. Girl, that has already been established, I think to myself. Touché.

***

444 Roger Boulevard

"Baby, baby, ba-by, give me one reason why we can't fuck…It's been two months now?" That dreamy man Dick-String-A-Long sure has a way with words as well as a hungry look in his eyes.

Oh-no, I think to myself. *I knew it! Uh-huh. I knew it! I knew that he was gonna crack. What a wimp.* I turn to look away tapping my foot, quite annoyed. "Because." I reply, with my back facing him.

He gently grabs my slender arm and turns me around to face him. "Is that a legitimate reason? C'mon, baby." His sweet breath blows in my face. After witnessing no change of heart in me, his toned arms rise mid-air and fall like light flurries on a wintry day. Then he walks in front of the door of 444 Roger Boulevard, blocking the exit to his luxurious bachelor's pad almost like he is forbidding me to leave.

At this point I have had enough of the drama for one evening. "Move." I huff, as I put my weight on my right leg and cross my arms about my chest with a sulk plastered on my face, rotating my left heeled pump in his burgundy plush carpet, and flinging my Beverly Johnson weave off my left shoulder.

This tower of a man draped in his silky black pajama bottoms crosses his bare feet and arms in a defiant stance. "Not until you give me one reason." His bedroom eyes pierce mine. My body flashes with warmth and my mind is in a flustered state. Immediately, I feel trapped.

Slowly, I can feel the pressure in my chest heaving to give in, but the stubbornness in me won't back down. My forefinger sways cutting the thick film in the air and I speak in my child-like voice. "Look, I can give you twenty-seven reasons but none would be sufficient. We've talked about this and you said…" I stop talking because it is a waste of good breath. I cut my almond-shaped eyes up to the ceiling avoiding the look on his dark-skinned face. Oh, that handsome face of his makes me wet. Lord. That face makes my insides drool. *Keep your eyes to the ceiling, girl.* That face makes my stomach knot and my toes curl in my pumps. That face makes my nipples hard as rocks. *Keep staring at the ceiling.* That face makes my heart race, mouth water, and pulse rise. *Don't back down.* That face makes me remember a time when I would've given anything to be with him intimately, but I am not the same woman as before. *That's right state your claim!* Things have changed. I have changed. I live a life of celibacy and any man who wants to be in my circle has to respect my choice. *If he only knew*, I think. If only.

Darn, he is fine. His handsome features distract my thoughts. Slowly I step closer toward the door, but his solid frame continues to block my way. His hands surrender to be heard, "Listen Kake, can't we compromise? Can't we discuss this calmly? We are both adults here. Look, I'll try harder but you gotta cut a brotha some slack." *Is he whining? I know he is not whining. Kake, listen to what the man has to say.* "Kake, you are a beautiful woman. This isn't easy for a man like me. Damn, baby I just got home from work. So what I want to make love to my woman." He cracks a smile showing off his ivory-colored teeth. Within a couple of minutes I take the stick out of my derriere and ease up a bit. I nod my head up and down. "Okay, we'll try this dating thing again Saturday night."

"Deal." He massages those massive hands together as his size thirteen feet step aside and open the door for his favorite girl to walk out with my head in the friggin' clouds.

Bridgette Complex (Apt 2A)

Kake. That's me. The girl Dick String-A-Long has had a crush on since his baptism. Since kindergarten. Since Sunday school. Since fourth grade. Since high school. Since college. Since the time he saw my toffee-colored face glow in the hot sun at Great Adventures while I was puking my brains out after riding on the roller coaster. It was then that I knew that he was meant to be mine and I his. But some things don't always go as planned. He won and I lost. What I mean by that is he got tired of waiting for me to get tired of waiting for the "right time" to come so he moved on with life, met someone compatible, and got engaged. Talk about tough blow. It was hard to accept once I got word, but I felt at fault. I let time skip by and he let *her* enter his life. Yes, I lost the man I dreamed to marry, have children with, and grow old with. I lost a good apple. I lost because I took too long to decide what I wanted. I let work take control of my life. I let churchgoers influence me. I let arrogance dictate that he would never get tired. That he would wait for me because he loved me so. He loved me so much that he let me go. And now I sit dry and dreary wondering when my prince charming is going to tie-the-knot with *her*. I don't know her name and I don't care to know. I screwed up because I overly thought about this and that. About the fact that I had two daughters played a major part in my decision-making. He could never understand the pressure he put on me. I mean he vowed to be my daughter's stepfather, but I had to be sure that he would be a good role model in my children's life, especially after the unexpected death of their biological father, Benny. He was a good loving boyfriend and father. He looked so much like Mario Lopez. Unfortunately, due to his untimely and unexpected death my life changed seemingly overnight. All it took was one stray bullet to take him from my daughters, Mia and Maya and me. They were too young to remember him, but often I talk him up so that they will know a little about him. Things were moving so fast in our lives. Somewhere I lost faith because of all the negativity that was surrounding and suffocating me. So I let the man that I have loved forever get away. Now…now I *am* settling with Done. I have no problem admitting the truth. I am settling for a man I have no deep feelings for. Why settle, I keep asking myself that same question. But my baby sister, Thelma seemed to answer it so profoundly when she said, *"Sis, settling for a man can be your happiness."* I pondered over her words. *Maybe she's right. Maybe she's wrong.* There is only one way to find out, I thought to myself. I remind myself that the man I stood by was not Dick. It was Done Deal. Darn. I daydream about Dick every time I am in Done's presence. I guess this is how it is when you are not committed: mind, body, and soul to the person. What choices do I have? I shrug my shoulders. All I can do is live this love triangle out and see who comes out living in fairytale bliss—Dick with me or Me with Done. What a tangled web. And it gets worse because all I keep imagining is *her* sinking her teeth in my good apple. *My* meant-to-be-mine-man.

WHITE KITTY

657 Groover Way

My cell phone ring, ring, *rinnnnggggggggggggggs…*

"He-llo." I moan seductively with my legs wrapped around *her* smooth as silk back. "Done?" I try to compose myself, scratch my throat to distract the background music of her tongue licking my twat, but the feeling. Damn, this feeling is so f-in' good I wanna scream out her name. "Yeaaaahhhh. Ah, it's two o'clock in the morning. This betta' be gooddddd."

"Twat, baby, I miss you. Can't we talk about this?"

I sigh. "Maybe."

"Look, my gurl and I are on the verge of parting. I need to feel you. Damn, I miss you."

My forehead crumples. "You are a trip, you know."

"What do you mean?"

"I'm sayin' you swagger around like you're god's gift and shit. You got somebody and you don't even appreciate her, yet, you want me. Damn, how greedy can one be?" I bat my lashes from the feeling she is giving me.

"Listen, I am willing to try harder. I miss your rain," he says.

"Yeah, I miss it too." I part my lips dying to moan. "I, I, I...I gotta go."

"Aiight."

As I am placing the phone back in the cradle Synthetic stops licking my twat and looks up at me with those Paris Hilton eyes of hers. "Who was that, Twat?"

"That's none of your concern, baby. Just keep doing what you are doing." I say followed by a moan echoing how good I feel inside. My eyes spread wide and then close as I feel the cream oozing out of me. I have to lie still to regain myself as I heave out deep breaths.

Synthetic is my white kitty. Yeah, I met her at *Lipstick on my Collarbone*. This was around the time I promised myself that I was through with men, including Whupp. But as you know that was a white lie. Synthetic is a phony bitch. That's where her stripper name comes into play. She is sexy, though. I love that fact that she is a freak in the bedroom. After Synthetic pleased my kitty she gets up to go take a shower while I lay sprawl across her bed.

Minutes later my cell phone rings, again.

I roll over and answer it. "Hello."

"What's my pussy up to?"

"Done?"

"Your's truly."

"Oh, nothing."

"Well, I'm coming over so that I can lick that pussy."

I kinda like it when he is aggressive. I hope he has some tricks up his sleeve.

"Sorry, luv, but I'm not home."

"Where you at?"

"At a friend's house."

"Who? 'Cause since I've known you you have never had any friends, especially female friends."

I smirk. *This nigga thinks he knows me, huh.*

"Where you at Twat?"

"At a friend's house."

"Twat, stop playin' wit' me, okay."

"I'm at this bitch Synthetic's house."

"Oh, what you fucking bitches now or something?"

Silence. Then I chuckle.

"Oh, oh, that's funny or something." Done says, "What's that bitch address? Shit, I'll fuck both of y'all."

"Oh, no the hell you won't!" I snap.

"What's the bitch address, Twat? You know you want this big dick."

Damn, he got me there.

Slowly, I give in. I mean I can't turn down a big dick. "Okay, it's 657 Groover Way."

"I'll be there shortly."

I roll my eyes. "Whatever."

We hang up.

"Synthetic, Synthetic, Synthetic!" I yell from the bedroom.

"Yeahhh."

"You better get a move on. You don't want to lose your gig at *Lipstick on my Collarbone*. You know how Zeek is."

"Yes, you're right. If I'm late he'll want me to suck his nasty ass dick. I can't stand that fat muthafucker."

Synthetic hurries to get dressed, grab her bag, and places my money on her nightstand. That's right. Pussy ain't free! She sprints out the door nearly breaking her neck in those six-inch stilettos. I chuckle.

Twenty minutes later, there is a ring at Synthetic's doorbell. I get up off the bed; walk downstairs to open the door. Done stands before me his white Coogi sweat suit with tan Timberland boots on with a grin on his boyish face. It is obvious that he has been drinking because I can smell the Grey Goose Vodka on his breath.

I frown. "Damn, how much did you have to drink?"

Done crack a smile. "Just a few shots."

"Shit. You smell like you had more than a few." I say. It is a complete turnoff for me.

"Baby, c'mon. Don't start bitching, okay. I just wanna stick my dick up in you to calm your fine ass down."

"I'm calm. Trust me." I say, almost laughing in his face. I have already been fed but I am willing to have seconds as long as he can keep his dick up. I slip out of my T-shirt; pull down my thong, and push Done on the bed. I unlace his Tims, pull them off along with his sweatpants and boxers, and there standing tall is his trophy for me to honor with my glossy lips. Done leans his inebriated self-back and let's me pleasure him. The wetness from my tongue arouses him quickly. Immediately he let's out a, "Shittttt, damn, fuck!" all in one breath. That is a turn on for me. I am already dripping rain down my legs. Oozing with sex juice as his dick gets thicker and harder. I rise to my feet and ride him into a peaceful sleep. That muthafucker starts snoring and shit. All I can do is smile. I am not even mad. It is kinda cute watching him curl in a ball, but I have to wake his ass up before Synthetic happens to come home early.

I let Done sleep for an hour longer and then I wake him up, suck his dick again, and then say, "Mommy, loves you." And peck his *head* before he slips *it* in his pants and tucks him away. Then I send Done on his merry little way. And then I take my ass home to my hubby.

CRACK DAT ASS!

444 Roger Boulevard

Mid-November. The door squeaks, as Dick String-A-Long, stands behind me waiting for me to just walk into his condo. My feet are planted outside the door pretending to be stubborn so that he will spoil me rotten by taking me by the hand and us walking in together, as a gentleman should. Every lady wants to be treated as such and I am no different. I must've been daydreaming for a split second 'cause Dick was far from being a gentleman this particular day. "Twat, go ahead in." Dick says. I sigh, and then walk in his residence.

Dick has too much street in him and it shows on his outer, but that wasn't the reason I decided to take a chance with him. No. The bad boy mentality had been played out for me a long time ago. I am not interested in him for that, and plus, that isn't quite his style.

Maybe back in the day, I could see it. I don't know how to quite describe him but bad boy doesn't fit the bill. Not with Dick.

After over fifteen years of trying to grasp my attention I decide to see what this dark-skinned Muslim man, who stands about six two with a washboard stomach is all about. Deep within my stomach I think I already know. I just want confirmation of what that little voice spoke of years ago. Back then, it told me "not yet." And it was saying the same thing, but it added, "well see what he is about," but then it said "not serious about you so enter at your own risk" and "like it or not 'cause this man ain't ready to settle down even though he claims he's looking for a "decent" woman." Already he has me confused. Okay, either you want a relationship with someone or you don't. Make up your mind. I can't stand a flustered-mind-brotha' who thinks a woman wants to hear "commitment" all the damn time. Not all women want to settle down and lie on our backs and have babies. Some of us have passed that stage in our lives and we just want to be wanted, if only for a few hours out of the day. Some of us just want the fuckin' truth without the added bullshit because it is just a waste of time when we could be doing better things like getting our fuck on, you feel me? Just cut through all the bullshit and *come* correct. That's what I like. A brotha' who can lay down the law and keep my pussy lips clapping. That's the kind of happy I want. Treat me well and I will do my damnedest to make you feel like fuckin' Godzilla. With all of this experience I got I can make a man fall in love with me. But I ain't trying to go there because I am in a complex situation, and plus, love hurts too much for me. But if I am plotting to have him fall deeply in love with me this is what I would do.

Give him *head* everyday!!!!! I'd suck his dick for hours until the skin turns raw.

My feet enter the chilly room, which is his bedroom. The first name that come to mind is "Booty-Call" simply because that is the first room you enter, but Dick says that he had a roommate and he hadn't had a chance to switch the rooms back. The bedroom is actually the living room. I can't say whether I believe him or not because he seems a little sneaky. I think he's a lady's man. And honestly I don't think one woman can satisfy him. But I ain't trying to go there. I just want to have fun. I must admit it feels kinda awkward and it makes me feel a bit uncomfortable because what does that say about me. I have already waltzed in "Booty-Call" and honestly I don't want to leave in a hurry. I kinda enjoy his company. I want and hope to get to know Dick a little better. I mean since my last never-gonna-do-this-again rendezvous I figured men, not all, but most were not looking for anything meaningful even if their mouth spoke of it. Most of the time that was during cuddling, kissing, or fucking that those lies would spew out in lust talk. It was all lies. And eventually the lie would come to light when our bodies would cool down. That's when the "I dunno-what-you-are-talkin'-about" comes into play. Yes, the amnesia. Like they don't remember a damn thing. With Dick I am not quite sure as to what he wants with me, but I know that it isn't just to talk or watch cable, as he'd claimed. I am open to see what this man is really about. I mean damn, he has chased me for soooooooo long I figured being *caught* would make things a bit more interesting or not.

Truthfully, Dick is a bit immature for his age. He is always blurting out, "Crack kills!" *And* I'd ask what does that mean. He simply says, "One minute you are tired, but you keep getting up and down, down and up, running to the bathroom like fifty times, putting your clothes on, taking your clothes off. You act like a restless crackhead." And then he'd chuckle like that was something a lady wanted to be depicted as. Dumb ass! So you can understand why I can't seem to pinpoint the age of this young man, but I think between 26-30. His features remind me of a straight-faced politician (*and everyone knows politicians are liars*) all suited in a gray-pinned striped suit with a briefcase in tow. Why he reminds me of that I don't really know. Dick seems interesting to me, and for the most part I hope for something better than the last dog that dragged himself out of my life. All I can do is hope. Dick seems to know what he wants and how he is going to get it. That I like about him. He seems genuine in wanting to help people in the black community. I know that from him being a coach for the little league teams. He seems grounded, and that I like too. There are some good qualities about him that make me want to explore. I love his cleanliness for one. Being on his job for several years as a substance abuse counselor shows stability and owning his home shows responsibility. He drives a practical car. But it is not the material things that grasp my attention with Dick, not at all. I have grown tired of the same old fuck-ups and I am diligent about seeing something new and seasoned as far as an experienced man who knows how to treat a lady. I mean he talks a good sermon, but he has a tendency to twist his words into making you think one thing when honestly he means another. I need to see firsthand what this man, Dick String-A-Long can bring to the table. Can he give me something *unique*? I don't see it in him, but I am hoping that it is buried somewhere beneath that long pipe that dangles between his legs. I am hoping it is dying to *come* shining out in my presence.

(I'm going to keep this as real as I can).

Prior to this Dick called me earlier. It was like 7:00 in the morning, if I'm not mistaken. He said that he had been trying to contact me. That same day was when he'd asked me out to go to the movies that coming Friday.

Okay, Friday had come and Dick and I met at a disclosed location and then we went to the movies. I wore my halter multi-colored dressed with stilettos and shawl to wrap around my arms should the night air get nippy. We had dinner at I-HOP because the movie started later than we anticipated. There we were in the movie theater and Dick kept feeling on my thigh. It made me feel uneasy so I had to keep moving his hand and I distracted him by pecking him on the lips. Obviously Dick needed some attention.

After the movie Dick took me back to our disclosed location. And quite honestly I was eager to get home because the "date" wasn't a fulfilling one for me because I had so much on my mind, and plus, I wasn't really big on Dick.

Sometime after that Dick asked to stop by our disclosed location and I said no that I'd meet him at his place. We watched DVDs. I remember we kissed. I wanted a bottle of wine but Dick stated that he didn't drink but once I arrived he went to get me a bottle of Sangria. We cuddled on his chenille covered garnet-colored sofa. Then Dick's phone rang, but he didn't answer it and that kinda got me annoyed. Okay, I knew that he was "kickin' it" with some female. How serious were the two? That I didn't know but I knew that they were knocking boots based on what he'd told me. Yet, he was telling me that he would stop seeing her if he could be with me because he always admired the way I carried myself. Like the lady I am. That was a turn-off for me, not the compliment, but the call. Finally I left not feeling the desire to see his fine ass again.

Unexpectedly, I received a call from Dick. It was a big surprise. He asked could he see me and I met him at The Baker's Lounge in my hometown of DeWitt. Still, it was something about him that got under my skin. The night with Dick was somewhat peaceful. We kissed and cuddled. He got me a bottle of White Zinfandel and I lay back and tried to relax. That wine had me relaxed, all right. So relaxed that our clothes came off and Dick and I had shared a night. Our first night of fucking was a memorable one for Dick because I left a lasting impression on the bed. With so much built up in me I had an orgasmic flush of relief all over Dick and the sheets. We most definitely needed some towels. All I could do was sigh after because it was way overdue. Hell, I hadn't had an orgasm in less than 6-hours. Of course, Dick thought I had peed on him, which I didn't. It took the edge off and I felt okay with things. Nothing serious, you know?

But by the next day, Dick had not called and that through a monkey wrench in my ego. I was annoyed. At least call to say what's up, hello, whatever, you know what I'm sayin'? Well, I took the initiative and called Dick (something I normally don't do) just to say how are you. (See this was the reason why some men thought that I was "controlling" "spoiled" and "want things my way" but that was not totally true. I would want to be treated as I treat him. I wouldn't want him feeling like a piece of meat so why not be the bigger person and just call to say something. I didn't see anything wrong with that. It did not state that we were on the verge of getting married, shit. It's all about respecting the agreement.) The agreement. We fuck, suck, lick, and call to keep the shit flowing.

Sex#2:

The next time I heard from Dick was either that next Friday or Saturday. We got together. We went to Microcomputer because he wanted to price some computers because his hard drive was on the verge of crashing. We stopped at nearest supermarket and packed up on some groceries and then headed to our spot at the Baker's Lounge. Dick made me a sandwich and I retrieved the bottle of wine I had left in his trunk. We made out on the sofa, which led to screwing on the bed like two wildlife animals in heat. It was so passionate. I called him Monday and I got his voice mail. I called him Tuesday and I also saw him ride right passed me as I was talking to this chick named Christmas, someone Bernetta (departed sister) used to hang with back in the day. Christmas looked like shit. All dried up and smelling like a brewery. Eyes all puffy and her skin were discolored with blotches about her face, neck, and upper arms. She looked bloated from the liquor. She bluntly told me that she was getting her "trick" on to support her cocaine habit. If she knew like I knew the bitch needed to stop while she was still standing 'cause soon her as would be six feet under. Anyway, Dick didn't beep his horn. That day I really got annoyed and I called him and blacked da fuck out on him. His response, "Damn, we just saw each other. What I'm 'sposed to call you every day?" I couldn't believe my ears. It was that difficult to pick up a phone just to say hello. You gotta be kidding me, I said to myself. I was heated that day. Heated!

A couple of days had passed. It was Thursday. I had recently joined a gym. (Gotta keep the body tight.) Actually I was about to head home to my dear hubby when my cell phone rang. It was Dick. He said he would like to see me. I said okay because I had cooled down by this time. He came to pick me up. I needed to go to the bathroom so I asked him to drive down to the nearest fast food restaurant. Dick parked his car but said something out of the way because I had brought up what was troubling me about his fucked up ways. Of course, the amnesia kicked it and it annoyed me even more. But what really got under my skin and fired me up inside was when Dick told me to shut up. I cut my eyes sharp and said, "What did you just say?" He turned his head to the side and said, "Twat, why you trippin'?" Now, we were on our way to the Westfield mall so that he could purchase some boots and after we were going to head to get a bite to eat, (his treat of course). Oh, I don't have a problem treating a man to dinner, okay. But I had a major problem with Dick's "shut up." Well, I got out of Dick's car and I walked inside Wendy's and I went to the bathroom, washed my hands, and had walked out the front door, passed him sitting in his car, and sashayed straight back to my car that was parked in the gym's parking lot. That's right! I left Dick parked by Wendy's still waiting for me to come out. Fuck him!

About a few days later while I was at the gym somebody touched my shoulder. Believe it or not it was Dick stating that he was still parked by Wendy's waiting for me to come out. I chuckled. And so did he. That had broken the ice between us. I was hoping that he would see that I was different. So what I was a younger woman, meant that I surely was not going to accept being disrespected by this asshole; I had enough of that from men. Those days were over for me. Over! That same day we went to the Baker's Lounge and got our fuck on.

Sex#3

November 15th I had called Dick because I couldn't sleep and I really needed someone to talk to. Okay…okay. I wanted to get my fuck on. He wanted to pick me up and bring me to his house, but it was too late for me to be going out especially since Whupp was home. So he suggested that I call him the next day, and we could meet then.

The next day I called Dick around 9:00 a.m., and we met at the Baker's Lounge. We watched cable, kissed, and cuddled. We laughed a little. I snuggled under the blanket and closed my eyes for brief moments. Then we had wild and crazy sex. We echoed vulgarity that would make your grandmother turnover in her grave. The bed squeaked for mercy. Our bodies were smacking together like hands clapping. Our juices were kissing up a friggin' storm.

I didn't call the next day to say hello to Dick. I waited the following day and I left a message. I actually didn't talk to Dick until November 22 around 11:00 a.m. That particular day I had some questions to ask him.

"Hello." Dick answered in a sleepy voice.

I cut to the chase. "Would you prefer I not call you?" I asked, ready to move the hell on with someone worthwhile.

"Nah. I don't have a problem with you calling. Us chillin'. We friends. It's just that I don't want to be in a committed relationship. I don't want to fall in love. And you, shit you will make a nigga fall in love with your freaky ass."

"I don't talk about us being together. You do, while we are slapping skins. It could be just your way of enhancing our foreplay. I don't bring any of that stuff up because I am too busy to be falling in love with anyone. I have a husband at home, as you already know. I don't have time to be playing juvenile games. I am certainly too young for that."

"Twat your mind is too sharp to be trying to get over on you. I wouldn't even think of it. I'm sorry if I made you feel like that. I'm not playing with you. But I don't want a "committed" relationship right now."

"Who said anything about "commitment" that is the farthest thing from my mind. I'm not asking you for one. I'm just letting you know how you make me feel, that's all. I just want to be treated nicely, respectful. Well, let me let you go." And that I did. I let him go up until it started to get hot again.

***

Dick rose early, probably around 7:00 a.m. I was wrapped in the comforter snoozing away. The TV was muffling voices. The fan was on. The door to the porch was ajar as Dick gazed out of the window inhaling the scent of new day. He returned back into the bedroom and got back in bed. I rolled over and snuggled up against his warm body. Our eyes spoke 'good morning' because our breaths were kicking. His chin caressed my head. And the chemistry between us led to a morning of "breakfast" in bed.

After our morning of passion, I took a shower. I remember before getting in the shower, I stared in the mirror and smirked. It felt good having someone there for me in *my* time of need. I stepped my nude body in the shower and let the water drench me as I inhaled the smell of peace. Dick's home felt just that way--peaceful.

After taking my shower, I exited the bathroom to find Dick reading his Father's Day card and placing it on his living room coffee table. "I see you're reading your card. Do you like it?" He looked up at me, "Yeah, baby, I like it a lot." His response made me feel so good inside. I tiptoed on the balls of my feet back into the bedroom. Dick resumed back to the bedroom as well. His sat and then stretched his body out on the bed with his back resting on the fluffy pillows. His eyes were engrossed in the TV. A few minutes later he rose to take his shower. I could hear the water running as I lotion my body down with Johnson's baby oil gel and put on my undergarments. I stretched my arms overhead and put on a white sleeveless summer top, while squeezing into my holey stretch jeans, but before I zipped them up Dick was entering the bedroom in his birthday suit beaded in moisture. He stood in front of the dresser mirror and massaged his body with baby oil gel, as he felt rejuvenated from the water. Then out of the blue he blurted out. "That's hot!"

"What?" I asked, still maneuvering my hips in my jeans.

"The candle. Yo, baby, I'm feelin' that." he said with enthusiasm.

I smiled because I felt the little I did paid off.

He turned towards me as he stood in front of the TV, "Lemme see you get in those jeans. Go ahead and jump up and down. You know how you women do. Go ahead and lemme see."

I chuckled, a little embarrassed.

"You can't get 'em up, can you?"

I just smirked, fidgeting around in the one space I occupied waiting for him to turn away so that I could inch my hips little by little until I was able to zip them up. Dick caught me and burst out laughing. It was pretty funny so we both burst out into laughter. He really made my day, until he opened that mouth of his and spoiled what could've been a wonderful day. For some reason the fact that I was comfortable in his presence bothered him in a way that he would sabotage the moment. I guess the closeness; the connection put some fear in him. His only recourse against us becoming closer was to build this wall and cause havoc as his weapon to push me away.

Dick picked me up. Usually we'd spend time together (it seemed) when it was convenient for him. I took the ride because I started to feel something special for him. And I thought. Oh, it doesn't matter what da fuck I thought.

When I would go over to his house I would get comfy. I would immediately strip down to my thong feeling free and liberated as I stretched my legs out on his bed and engrossed my eyes in TV. Dick and I snuggled on the bed. Like I said everything felt right to me. But to him I can't speak on his behalf. His hand caressed my thigh and eased up to my protruding nipples. His moist mouth massaged it with his slimy tongue. My head tilted back. Eyes closed inviting him in to have his way with me. And I'd automatically become submissive. Yearning to be touched with care and compassion. He delivered long passionate strokes that lifted my legs up and my feet landed on his back. His rhyme was smooth like a sharp edged knife. I'd moan. As he'd sang, "Oh, shit," at least ten times in one breath. Almost each stroke he'd cuss to let me know how good it felt being b'tween my legs. I felt all seven inches of him. Deep, so deep that I thought his dick would come outta my ass. He knew how to work his dick. How to maneuver it to bend, curve, and suction my wet twat. He knew how to pleasure my mind and body. He knew how to put me in hypnotic daze. He knew how to calm my anxiety. He knew how to comfort my soul and nurture my spirit. He knew all these things that no one had ever delivered to me. How could I not be swept in this beautiful place of unfamiliarity? How could I not?

Being with him I only climaxed twice. Once being on top. I liked to be in control. This particular day I let all of my inhibitions flow out of me and on to his stomach. Splashing like rain on dry pavement. Splashing on to his dick and balls and the bed sheets. All were drenched in my love juice. Drenched! The other time he'd made me climax was when he teased my clitoris. The motion of his finger, slow and fast rippled these waves of stimulating sensation throughout my whole body. God it felt so good. It felt good to feel him inside of me too. The stillness was poetic. Each word he spoke brought me back to the here and now. Dick was feeling extra good that day when he said, "Baby, that was fly!" as I laid back and stared at him and eased out a deep breath I was beyond satisfied. Beyond content. What I was feeling was far beyond anything that I'd ever felt in my entire life. A bitch was falling.

(In case you're wondering about Whupp. Well, I told him that I was going on a bus ride to Atlantic City).

***

6:54 a.m.

Dick had taken an early shower. I turned on my side. With one eye barely open I asked, "Baby, why are you up so early?"

He turned to me as he was rubbing down his left leg with Johnson's baby oil gel. "I felt sticky." God he smelled so good. I, on the other hand, was funky. I had crust in the corners of my eyes. My armpits were humming of musk. My coochie was more than likely humming fishy-woo-woo. Regardless of this, we always had "breakfast" in bed. And that morning was no different from any other. Showered or not the passion was never waived. It was more enhanced. More delicious than if we'd both smelled like KoKomusk oil.

Dick settled down and stretched his body horizontal on the bed. His left arm scooped under me as he rolled on top of me. Funky or not I'd never deprive the man. I wouldn't withhold sex for selfish reasons. I wanted him just as much as he wanted me.

The sexual chemistry was uncanny. I mean I saw stars. Bright stars. I saw candlelit nights with us wrapped in an afghan lying on a sandy Malibu beach inhaling the sea salt. I felt the ocean waters against my supple skin. I saw the sunrise in his eyes—the moon smiling back at us in such bliss.

It was a magical day. It was a day that I became bolder and even more confident than I had ever been. I didn't fight the urge to *expose* myself. No. I welcomed it with open arms. I spoke words that melted from my heart—words that had been hibernating within. Living stagnant within my soul. I spoke. I spoke. Me. The liberated woman! "Baby, look at me." I said softly as I lay in between his legs. Those lukewarm legs of his kept my temperature rising. I sniffed in his alluring scent that had me sloppy moist. "Look, into my eyes." His eyes pierced mine, hard. My mouth opened. I swallowed once. And then I said in softness, "I'm falling in love with you." Those sincere and beautiful words made him feel uneasy. Slightly mystified. Unguarded. Oblivious. Special. He struggled with the words. There was a battle forming within himself. Yes, I felt and saw it. Stared lively into his eyes. He looked at me. "I love you, too." he said with a straightness of face. I smirked. "But you're *not* in love with me." His autumn-brown eyes pierced mine, again. "Twat, I care deeply for

86

you. I love you. I would be there if you ever needed me. I would never hurt you (intentionally). I love you." Enough said, I thought. I wasn't disappointed. I was content. I felt free. "Dick, I could die tomorrow, but at least you know. You've heard it from me. You know I look at life with a fresh pair of eyes. These days I don't want to hold anything back. I'm learning how to free my soul. To say how I truly feel regardless of the outcome. I want you to know that I've fallen in love with you, Dick. You've wanted me for nearly twenty years of your life—of my life. This…this is the final outcome. I'm here. Finally, I'm here." He just stared at me in disbelief, and in deep thought. I could visibly see a look of: *I'm not ready. I dunno. Commitment. Wow. So soon.* Cast over his handsome face.

In my mind, it wasn't too soon. It had been nearly twenty years. It's okay, I thought. At that moment flashes of past, of another pair of sheer legs: mocha, butterscotch, caramel, chocolate, pecan, and white chocolate, laughter smothered the room, seductiveness saturated the air, sound effects of moans and groans, fingers taunting and teasing, hands and fists gripping and squeezing the bed sheets, tongues licking and his dick stroking *her* inward and outward crossed before my eyes. Face(s) of silhouette danced around in my head. Lying where I lay. Feeling what I felt. Tasting what I tasted. Naïve, I was not, but fallen in love… was I.

I lay my head on his warm chest and I closed my eyes blocking the face(s) out. Everything felt right after the images faded away. From the calmness in his bedroom to the sound of birds chirping, the breeze from the fan, and the touch from his hands, it all felt right. I was no longer afraid to feel *good*. Finally I was in the right place. At least, I thought I was. "There is no timing when it comes to matters-of-the-heart. It is what it is, Dick. At least you know." I said, again. "I'm at peace, baby. I'm at peace with how I feel." Then I thought *my time might not be his time. I mean he'd lived his life and so have I. We've crossed paths and here we are. But just as he waited I guess I have to do the same. Questioning myself is he worth the wait? I don't have an answer for that at this moment. Regardless, of what I am currently feeling the universe is what kept our connection burning. Patience is what kept our desires hungry.*

After "breakfast" I took a shower. I got dressed in my white linen pants and white wife beater T. I slipped on my gold Steve Madden sandals. Put on my rope earrings that dangled to my neckline. Dick followed suit and pulled out a short set and pulled out the iron and iron board. I pulled off my linen pants and ran the iron across them to get some of the wrinkles out of the pants leg. Then he ironed his clothes and took another shower.

Dick returned back to the bedroom while I was primping in the mirror. "Ah, shit, I'm feelin' that, baby!" he bellowed with excitement. I smiled. "You look like Pam Grier, baby." he embellished. I chuckled. Eventually Dick was fully dressed. He walked out to the short distant hallway and put on his black sneakers, reached high on top of the armoire and grabbed a black baseball cap, grabbed his keys, turned off the TV, and we headed out for a real breakfast at I-Hop on Route 151.

We waited about fifteen minutes before I hear, "Twat…party of two." Dick and I stood as the hostess escorted us to our *favorite* table. A few minutes later this chipper young man who looked every bit of eighteen or nineteen years old greeted us. His ash-brown buzz cut was neat as well as his attire.

"Hi. I'm Zachary. What would you two like to order?" he concluded his sentence with a bright smile.

We gave Zachary our orders and he grabbed the menus off the table and walked away. Probably about fifteen minutes later Zachary came back with our food. I had a spinach omelet without mushrooms and pancakes and tea with lemon and honey. Dick had beef sausages, three boiled eggs, grits, pancakes, I think? I know he ordered his favorite breakfast beverage: Pepsi. And if I'm not mistaken he ordered a refill of Pepsi.

After breakfast, Dick stopped by his boys' way to pick up his teams trophy. He mazed through some side streets to hand out smaller trophies to his little league team members. Then he dropped me off in front of my door. "I had a nice time with you, baby." He said, as he turned and looked me in my face. I reached for the door handle to let myself out. "Gimmee a kiss," he asked. So I turned around before exiting out of his silver car and kissed him on the lips. "Call me, baby," he said. As I was exiting out of the car I said, "Okay," and smiled as I saw Whupp's car was not in the driveway. I was taking a huge risk but I didn't give a fuck. This day with Dick I felt so rejuvenated. So alive. So on cloud ten.

In my heart, I knew. I knew more than I divulged to know.

***

"Twat, I'm looking for a decent woman." Those very words of Dick reminisce in my head each time I recap our weekends together. *He says he's looking for a decent woman. Please.*

In my opinion, "decent" no longer exists, at least not with me.

Yeah. Suddenly, I had a change of heart. I mean I've tried numerous of times to be "her". Actually I didn't have to try too hard because I was once her—the romantic, the one who bought the negligees. Modeled them for him. Did the seductive strut. Made the booty clap. Took bubble baths with him. Showers together. Shared chocolate covered strawberries and sipped on Chardonnay on ice. I cooked and cleaned. Gave of myself. Loved him. Gave him *head* mostly every night, unless I was feeling under the weather. Catered to his wants and needs. Forgot about me. I'd come later. It's no big deal. Or so I thought. But that didn't seem good enough. No. He had to have "options". A variety of pussy to fuck on a whim. And I tried. I tried by ignoring the truth. Truth. That *bitch* made me sick! Well, the truth was one woman could not satisfy his libido called Black Shepherd.

Why? Why am I dealing with this? Twenty years. TWENTY years this man pursued me. Every time he'd ask me out, I'd politely say no. Every time he'd invite me to a movie, I'd say no. Every time he'd invite me out for dinner, I'd say no. Why did I say yes? Loneliness? Curious? Attraction? Something different? Timing? I'm not sure. Shit!

I have to ask myself: Twat, what does he see in you?" and I swear. I swear I couldn't answer the question. Sure I am beautiful, sexy, fun...and a freak behind closed doors, but what else does he see? *There is more to me.* Look, I have good reason to feel frustrations. See I let my guard down. C'mon...did I really think that he was interested in me for my mind? No. He wanted to fuck me crazy. Men. They are visuals. All they see is the physical, at first. Everything else seems to become a blur very quickly. I assumed. I guessed. (Sighing) I hoped that he would be different. God, I hoped and prayed a lot on that. I prayed hard.

But again, it seems I've been *had*. Had the dick now it's gone. Another failed lustship. (blowing hot air out of my mouth) I know. I knowwwwwwwww. I allowed my emotions to run free. I was buck-naked. I let that damn estrogen take the lead. My mind was thinking quickly and my mouth opened and the words started spewing out full force professing my feelings. I couldn't stop it. I didn't want to stop it. I figured. I assumed. I guessed. I had hoped that he would've been happy. I mean twenty years was a long time to be pursuing a woman. I thought he was looking for someone decent. Someone to love and love him back. I allowed my eyes to see him in a different light. Bright and promising. It must've been a dim light. I knew I needed glasses. It might be a good time for me to invest in a pair. My heart opened after all those years. I allowed the inner-woman feel again. I allowed her feel *good*. What I wouldn't do to feel that feeling again. And, and, I enjoyed the feeling, very much. I soaked in it. He made me feel wanted. And I wanted to feel wanted. Desired. Even loved, if possible.

I figured after twenty years there had to be something from both parties to invest in: time, patience, understanding, moral support, as well as good sex. I hoped that my curvaceous frame would entice him enough to want just me. And only me. I assumed. I guessed. I had hoped. I was furious! I should've kept my guard up high. But I didn't. I let him stroke me long and deliciously. I enjoyed every bit of him because at the time it felt soooooooo right. That's where I fucked-up. It felt too right. Too good to be true. I mean with all the fucking he was doing it sure did come to light on my ass.

277 Liverpool Way

I woke up around 7:30 a.m., feeling this pressure in my abdomen. Whupp is sound asleep. I don't know what is wrong with me. I grab a pair of jeans, white tank top, and my undergarments and head for the bathroom to take a shower. The pressure grows stronger so I sit on the toilet thinking it is something I ate from yesterday that didn't agree with me.

I pee. But when I wipe myself from front to back with the white tissue I see bright red. My eyes spread wide. Then I freak the hell out trying not to wake Whupp. Oh, shit!

Period? I no longer get my period because at the premature age of thirty-five I had a partial hysterectomy. I don't have a uterus. I have a cervix and ovaries so I know doggone well I ain't the P word: pregnant.

I wipe myself again—still more bright red. At first, I want to run out of the house and sprint to the hospital. But I have to at least wash my ass. I take a shower. Then get dressed slightly slumped over.

As I grab my bootleg Gucci bag that Dick had given me. I think to call him.

"Hello."

I don't hesitate with my words. "I'm bleeding." By now the

pressure is whooping my ass. "I'm on my way to the hospital. I just wanted to let you know." I say pacing the floor.

"You're bleeding? Whatchu got your period?"

Now how many times have I told this man I don't get that anymore?

"I don't get my period." I say in a crackling voice. Now I'm terrified because the pressure is even more intense. What's wrong with me? I head out the door to my car, but then I think to just take the bus because my car is too noticeable. I practically speed walk to get on the first bus smoking.

Damn!

I hop on the 684.

This middle-aged white man with salt-and-pepper hair drives like a snail because he is too busy flirting with this teenybopper with the hoochie skirt on, while the pain in my abdomen is whooping me good. I start rocking in my seat. In my mind I'm saying hurry up and get me to Houghton Street, please! Hit the gas! Hit the muthafuckin' gas pedal, man! But he's just cruising along.

Finally I *ding* for him to stop as I see House University and Medical Center across the street. I wish I could sprint over there, but the pain, the mutha-freakin' pain!

I approach the registry desk and speak with a white woman with short blond hair and glasses.

"I'm having pain in my abdomen. I'm spotting." I say, hovering over her desk.

"What's your D.O.B?"

I tell her while damned near whining out my words.

"Your address?"

Bitch, look at the computer screen. I know you see it, I think to myself.

"It is the same in your system," I say, but I recite it out."

"Have a seat in the two chairs inside by the door."

"Okay."

The pain!

I sit in the chair holding my stomach. I look around at everyone looking at me. I inhale. It smells like sick people. Duh?

Finally the triage nurse calls me in the room. "Mrs. Twat?"

I stand, still slightly slumped over as I walk into the small room. It is so damn bright.

The white man with blonde hair asks, "What seems to be the problem, Mrs. Twat?"

"I have pain, lots of pain. I'm spotting blood too."

He looks at me holding my stomach.

"In your lower abdomen?"

"Yes."

He stands in his blue scrubs and takes my blood pressure. By now the pain has increased.

"How much do you weigh?"

Shit, I don't know, I think to myself.

"Ah, maybe 115-120."

"Allergic to any medications?"

"Penicillin."

"How old are you?"

"40. Just kidding. I'm 60-something... Hon, you figure it out."

"When was your last period?" he asks as he hands me a plastic bag with a pee cup and a clear tube with white cap in it.

"When I was thirty-five."

He looks at me like I have a booger on my nose. I guess I should explain. "I had a partial hysterectomy when I was thirty-five."

He nods his head up and down.

Shit! Are we through?!

"You look very young," he says.

I reply, "I hear that all the time."

This skinny young looking Hispanic man with dark hair dressed in tan scrubs comes near the door entranceway and says, "Mrs. Twat? You can come with me when you're through."

When do I get to pee in the cup, I wonder.

The pain!

"Okay. Okay." I say.

This dark curly haired woman boldly interrupts the dark haired man. "I need her insurance information, first."

Oh, yeah, the hospital gotta get paid. I could drop dead any minute now but who cares.

The pain!

"Initial here. Sign you name here. Print your name here. Sign your name here. Sign your name here," she says, seeing that I am about to keel over if she don't hurry da hell up.

I nod to let the dark haired man know that I am ready. I gotta pee in the cup. Hurry up! I gotta pee-pee!

We walk through the hospital like it's a maze. We take the elevator up. Get off. And we enter this large spacious room of beds and long curtains for privacy.

"Ma'am, you can take bed six," the dark haired man says.

"Okay." I say, still somewhat hunched over.

I pace, pace, and pace.

I hear loud talking of men and women. Where is the doctor? I need a doctor! This black woman walks pass me and I pace and pace and pace. Suddenly, I really have to pee.

"Excuse me, where's the bathroom?" I ask this black lady dressed in a colorful smock.

She replies, "Out in the hallway."

Oh, Lawd. Will I make it out to the hallway, I wonder.

"Should I go ahead and pee in the cup," I ask the black woman.

She turns around. "Yes." she says, and vanishes out of sight.

Slowly I make my way out to the hallway. I knock to see if anyone is occupying the bathroom. I hear a woman's voice in the bathroom. She sounds Hispanic. I lean my right hand against the cool wall. My left hand I use to knock on the door. She says, "Somebody's in here," and she keeps on yapping away like she's sitting in the comfort of her home, while the pressure is kicking, kicking my ass even more. I already know that somebody is in there, but when the hell are you coming out? My body is jittery. The pain and pressure is treacherous. I can still here the woman gibbering on and on.

I pace, pace, and pace. And pace, pace, and pace. Finally, I hear a click. The bitch decides to take her ass back to work. She works at the hospital because she has on her blue scrubs. I drag my feet over to the one toilet. I proceed to tear open the plastic bag and reach in for the clear cup. I snap off the white cap. I position it just so underneath me to catch the urine that will be streaming out. Oh, the pain! That pain hits me sharp. As the urine is streaming out my eyes like to pop outta my head. What da fuck is that! Blood? Urine? I see something that looks like muddy pee-pee streaming out of me. *Oh, shit!*

I panic. So by now the panic is introduced to pain. I make my way to the sink and wash my shaky hands. I place the white cap on the cup. The clear tub I leave in the bag. I'll leave that for the nurse to do. I use my left foot to flush the toilet. I unlock the door and head back to bed six. I place the clear cup with muddy pee-pee on the table. Then I decide to pour the muddy-pee-pee in the skinny tube. So I do. I cap it and place both cups and tube in the plastic bag and try to relax my nerves, but I can't.

I hear people talking. I pace hunched over, hoping someone will come. I keep hearing them talk so I get annoyed and walk towards the voices. I say, "I have a cup of muddy-pee-pee. Something's wrong with me. Where is the doctor?" This young black man says,

"Mrs. Twat?" I say, "Yes." This white woman says, "I didn't know that you were here. Nobody told me. I'm sorry." Whatever. "Can someone see what the problem is? Something is wrong. That pee-pee should not be brown like that. Something is wrong." I say in a crackling voice. I return back to bed six, frightened.

Finally, the white rotund doctor with glasses and short blond hair dressed in a white lab coat comes to check me out. *About damn time,* I think. She speaks in some accent but I can still make sense of her words. She puts her hands on my stomach and gently presses down on my abdomen. I feel like I have to pee again. She looks at me and asks me some questions.

"When was your last period?"

"Thirty-five. When I was thirty-five." I squint my eyes and moan. "I had a partial hysterectomy."

"Do you have a fever?"

"I don't think so."

"Well, check your liver." she says. "I'll send someone to take your blood."

"Okay."

"Are you sexually active?"

"Yes." I say. *Aren't you,* I think to myself.

I feel slightly violated, but I know that she is only doing her job. *Twat lightens up.* I try to relax my nerves and body, but it is difficult to do. The pain!

This light-skinned woman with short crop cut comes into the room and turns on the TV.

"Chile, please." I say, while rolling my eyes.

She smiles.

The black lady in the colorful smock comes into the room to take my blood. This chick can't find a vein. *All the veins in my body and you can't find one! I'm really on edge.*

"Can you make a fist?" she asks. So I do. "What's wrong?" she asks. "Hell if I know I thought you knew." I say a bit annoyed. Finally she finds a vein. "Don't move," she says quickly. "Squeeze your fist."

Ouch, ouch, ouch!

Does she know what the fuck she's doing?

"Don't move," she says, again.

Where the hell am I going with muddy-pee-pee, lady? I'm mean c'mon.

I turn to look away. I hate needles with a passion. I feel woozy. My mouth is watery like I want to vomit, but I don't really want to.

Hurry up?

The black nurse in the colorful smock fills three clear tubes. As she is almost finished with the last one she places the cap on it and pulls out the needle from my arm. Blood spills all over the sheets. Blood dribbles down and around my arm. I feel dizzy. I feel like I want to faint, but I don't.

"Put pressure on your arm with this gauze," she says. So I do. The nurse covers the blood drippings with another white sheet. That's stupid, I think. I guess that's why they have Environmental Specialist to clean up their mess. Yuck! She leaves the room.

Five minutes later, this unfamiliar caramel-colored lady (nurse) comes with meds and a small cup of water in hand. She hands me three pills. One pill is percocet. I haven't eaten yet. But I take the pills anyway. I drown them with water and then I lay my body back and try to relax waiting for my blood results.

It seems like forever when the rotund doctor returns to my room. I was hoping that she hadn't forgotten about me. I feel woozy. High. I've never been high a day in my life, until now. I don't like the feelin'. What the hell! Oh, yeah, she did give me percocet. It's chilly so I pull the sheets up to my neck.

Finally. The rotund doctor returns. She ain't singing or humming or smiling. *Oh, shit!*

She stands before me with those glasses and those eyes burning through her lenses.

"Well," she says.

Immediately, I am panicking like a mutha-.

I feel like I wanna vomit. What's wrong with me?

Don't tell me. It's CANCER!
Don't tell me. I have Cancer!
It runs in my family. Oh, oh, oh!
Don't tell me. HIV!
Don't tell me. I'm HIV-positive!
Don't tell me. LUPUS!
Don't tell me. I have Lupus!
Don't tell me. HEART DISEASE!
Don't tell me. I have Heart disease!
Don't tell me. DIABETIES!
Don't tell me. I'm a Diabetic!
Don't tell me. MS!
Don't tell me. I have MS!
Don't tell me. SICKLE CELL ANEMIA
Don't tell me. I have Sickle Cell!

95

What do I have, Doc?

I come to.

"You're dehydrated," she says.

Exhaling.

"You have a bladder infection (urinary tract infection). You can get if from dehydration. Bacteria from sexual intercourse. Make sure after sex you go in the bathroom and flush your body out."

My eyes droop. *That dickhead...Dick! Yeah, I know whom I got this shit from—Mister Options man. But we had an agreement that if and when he decided to dip and dab that he would let me in on the secret. He knew, because I had stressed it more than once that when he decided that to exclude me out of the picture. Well, I guess he forgot to mention it. Yeah, okay. Breathe.*

The lady with the colorful smock returns with discharge paperwork and attached are three prescriptions:

(1) PERCOCET 5/325
DISPENSE #12 (TWELVE) Tablets. 1-2 tablets by mouth every 4-6 hours as needed for pain.

(2) 6 200 mg tablets
No refills.
    1 tablet 3 times a day.
    (medication should be taken with plenty of water).

(3) 14 Tablets
No refills.
    1 tablet 2 a day for infection.
    (medication should be taken with plenty of water).

I say thank you to the lady and walk down the hall, turn left to the elevator, and wait for it to come. Once I am on the G (ground) floor I head out the door to the outside world pissed off. I'm exhausted and high offa percocet. My body feels weird. Dick doesn't call. I call him. I keep my voice calm, mellow. But inside I am hot like fire.

"Hello."

"Yeah." he says. "What the doctor says?"

My eyes droop and darken.

"A bladder infection."

"Oh, that's good." he replies. "Where that come from?" he asks. "How you get that?"

I stare at my cell phone. This dickhead is *slowwwwwwwww.*

"Yeah," I add a hint of sarcasm. "Yeah, it could've been worse." *Boy, if I could reach through this cell phone I'd choke him. I wish I could grab his dick and dig my long nails in the pee-hole so he can feel how I feel. Ooh, I am mad!*

When I arrive home I lay down. Whupp comes up and asks me if I'm feeling sick. I say, "Yes, baby, it must be this damn menopause." as soon as I say the word *menopause* Whupp jets back downstairs. Finally I get some rest.

The next day, I don't hear from Dick so I call him. I call him: Tues, Thurs, and Friday. *Shouldn't this be the other way around? I'm the one sick, not him.*

Come Saturday I call him.

"Hello." he says.

"Listen, what I am 'bout to say to you I don't want you to get upset."

"Aiight."

"I don't know how many women you are fucking, but I would've thought that you would've used protection if you were stroking me. If you plan on continuing to see me, you need to change or this will happen again."

His response, "Right." and it is said rather nonchalantly. *I don't think he gets it.* Here I am fallen in love and this man is out fucking around. My heart kinda hurts.

I have a delay reaction Saturday evening. *Girl, you are blessed. You are blessed that he didn't give you an incurable disease. Or herpes, or anything, that would disrupt your life long-term.*

I thank God. But still embedded in my heart is a want and a sense of missing for this man. How much in love can I possibly be? Who do I love most: him or me?

Monday 10:09 a.m.

My cell phone rings.

"Hello."

"Can I speak with Twat?"

"Speaking."

"This is Dick."

"I know."

"How you know?"

"I know your voice."

"Oh." he replies. "I'm sorry for what happened."

"Uh-huh." I stare out of the window.

"I'm not ready for a committed relationship."

Well, I kinda figured that out with this infection and all. I know that you have a roaming dick.

"So what are you saying?"

"I can't give you what you want."

Might as well get some pleasure out of my pain by making him talk.

"And what do I want?" I ask cleaning underneath my fingernails.

"You and me."

"Oh. Listen, just because I express how I am feeling for you don't mean that I expect us to be on the verge of talking marriage. I just wanted you to know. But I told you this would happen. I told you you would change and you said no, now look. I'm the one suffering while you are out doing you."

"No. I'm just not ready. You're heavy." he says.

"I'm heavy. It's funny how you can want someone for twenty years and then you finally have the opportunity of having her. It is everything you could ever imagine it to be. You start feeling something different with this person. Then, you start trying to sabotage it because of your own deep feelings. Feelings that you don't want to feel, but you do. Twenty years you pursued me. I guess it was the challenge, the chase, huh?"

Silence.

"Listen, I still want us to do what we talked about," he says.

I cut my eyes to the side in disbelief.

Wait a minute. You don't want me but you want me to be your business partner. You want me to help you become successful while you gallivant around doing you.

"Wait." I have to wrap my head around this. "You still want to work with me?"

"Yes, baby. I mean Twat."

I smirk devilishly. "Let me ask you one question, with all the women you are fucking you mean to tell me that none of 'em you would want to do business with?"

He pauses, and then replies. "No. I want us to do it."

"Uh-huh."

Oh, I must be the one with the brains out of his "coochie clique." Or it could be that he just trusts me that much.

"Today would be a perfect day to meet. Say around 7:30 p.m." he says. "It shouldn't take long to get everything going."

"It will be overwhelming. It's not just a skip and jump transition. There's a lot involved in what you want to do."

"Yeah, yeah," he says, oblivious to what his business idea entails.

7:38 p.m.

My cell phone rings.

"Hello."

"Um, Twat, its Dick. Um, I'm not going be able to make it this evening."

"I kinda knew that from earlier."

"How'd you know?"

"Women's intuition." I say, ending it with a good-bye.

I sit back and think.

For twenty years this man has pursued me. And finally, finally I give in to see what he is all about. And in the end of it all, all I get is a lousy T-shirt that reads:

"FOR TWENTY YEARS HE PURSUED ME AND ALL I GOT TO SHOW FOR IT IS SOME MUDDY-PEE-PEE. Damn!"

***

After recuperating, I bounce back to the Twat I know. Already I find myself in a slight jam, though. Well, my twat is talking and won't shut da fuck up so I need some dick to stick in its mouth. I want the heiffa to shut up! She keeps whining and shit. "I'm hungry. Feed me." I need to do something to calm my nerves. I hate being stressed because it adds years on (you women know what I am talking about. One wrinkle and we are ready to slap a bitch.) I am fine and I want to stay this way.

Anticipating a late night out on the town I figure I'd call to see if Dick is in the mood for some *head* bopping.

"Hello."

"Hi. Um, were you busy?" I ask.

He sang a slow, "Yeeeeaaaahhhh."

The kind of yeeeeaaaahhh that made you *think* either he is engrossed in a TV show or in someone else's pussy.

"Oh. Well, I was gonna ask you, ah, but you said you're busy."

"Yeeeeaaaahhhh."

"Oh. Well, talk to you later."

Now, I can easily call Synthetic, but I am not in the mood for pussy tonight. I want something dark, thick, and manly. There is a couple of things I can do to ease some tension off. Get buck-naked and lay in the backseat and masturbate until I burst outside of myself. Or call Done. For some unknown reason, I decide to go to my car, park on a dark street, get buck-naked, and hop in the backseat with the Midnight hour on and pleasure myself. And that's exactly what I do. And it is the most exhilarating experience I have had in a long fuckin' time.

By the time I get home the house is pitch dark. Where's Whupp, I wonder. I exit my car; unlock my door, and step foot into a quiet house. There is a note on the living room TV stating that he stepped out with a buddy. The only buddy Whupp's has is Rufus White a middle-aged postal worker. Whupp grew up with Rufus and they have been friends for years. Rufus is divorced and is probably on the prowl for some new pussy to fuck. *They probably went to go play pool at the Billiard.* Okay, so that means I have the house to myself. Now, what could a girl like me get into while her husband was out hanging with his fellow friend? A lot.

***

It is Sunday. 5:30 P.M., and the February evening air is crisp. Whupp is out this particular evening, which is unusual because he is a homebody. The closets he'd come to going out is when he takes out the trash, checks the mailbox, or maybe if he is going golfing in the Catskills (up in the mountains) is really the only time he'd step out of the house. Most of the time Whupp is sitting in his olive-green Harlowe swivel recliner with his feet propped up on the ottoman and his eyes glued to the wide-screen Sony TV watching CNN, 20/20, or SNAPPED.

Well, I am feeling kinda freaky and I want to get my shit off. So it so happens that Done calls asking me to stop by his place. I jump at the offer. Put on something sexy and head out the door. Now, I know that Done can't always satisfy my needs, but he is such a gentle man and gentlemen are rare. Done is smooth and delicious. He is a dream for a woman like myself. It is his charm, his voice, his eyes, and especially his dick that keeps me coming back for more. So

I figure I'd school him on what it takes to keep my pussy wet. If he is willing to learn we can have a hell of a time. The choice I'll leave up to him. Of course, I know to entice him with the offer. You know, while I'm pecking his gem. There is no way that that man will turn down a good suck.

I park my Maximum a coupla blocks from Done's house. The streets are flooded with loud Spanish music, couples arm-to-arm, and women strutting in their pea coats with open toe sandals, skimpy skirts, and over-painted faces. The restaurants are full and lively, and cars tailgate slowly through the congested block. I swear I feel like I am in Manhattan. I stop at the nearest liquor store and ask Papi for a bottle of bubbly and two Slim Jims and pay and walk out. Then I head across the street and stop at the bodega for a box of Trogans. Then, I call Done on his cell phone to tell him to come open the door downstairs and hurry up because it is cold as hell.

The door squeaks open from the wintry air. Done stand in the doorway dressed in his fatigue shorts and wife beater looking all scrumptious and shit. He smiles that boyish smile that make my glossy lips spread into a smile.

"Come in," he says, with a grin painted on his face.

I smile, as I step inside inhaling the aroma of black bean chicken and rice. Pork chops. Empanadas, and some sweet scent I can't quite make out. Whatever it is it is making me hungry and not for food. Done leads the way to his room and I follow as I shut the door behind me. The room looks the same: four walls, window, cabinets, TV, chair, and all his shoeboxes lined up neatly. His iron board is lent against the white wall with a towel dangling. And his laundry bags lined up on the floor neatly stacked. The closet is full of his designer clothes just, as I'd remembered.

"Have a seat. Get comfortable. Take off your shoes. Hand me your coat," he says, while checking me out and hanging my coat on the leg of his iron board. "You look good, Twat."

He always seems to know exactly what to say. I told you he is smooth, I say to myself.

"I do?" I say. Of course I have to act like I don't know so that he can keep on saying it. I know it all along. Huh, I do look good because I take care of my body.

"I like those jeans." he says. "What are they, um?" he asks, as he leans back, crisscrosses his arms behind the back of his head and lies upon his palms like a pillow.

I smile. "No. Just jeans." I stare at that huge bulge growing in his shorts. Damn, it is huge. And it is begging for me to c'mere. I try to distract my thoughts by slipping my tongue out and sliding it across my lips.

"Ah, Done, do you have a bottle opener?" I pull the bottle out of the brown paper bag and place it on top of his stack of shoeboxes. Done stands to look in his cabinet drawer and then he go out into the hallway to check on top of the refrigerator. He comes back in as I am sprawled across his bed with nothing on but my hot Twat thong. Perky tits. Greasy nipples and my soaking wet pussy. My legs are spread eagle as my right hand eases down to my crotch and inches inside my thong, teasing my wet clit.

Done watches my every move as he drops the silver bottle opener to the floor and pulls down his shorts, drops his boxers, and walks over to the side of the bed and says, "Move over." He stands above me as he yanks on his rock hard dick; eyes glued to me watching me play with my sodden pussy. I stare him in his eyes and he stares into mine as we engage in pleasuring ourselves. It gets so intense that we both begin to moan loudly. Done groan simultaneously. Both of us are in our world of masturbating our hungry bodies to reach our climax.

Done's eyes droop as I open my legs wider, massaging my pussy as he listens to the wet music. He strokes his dick harder; eyes closed feeling the sensation build. I feel it too. I bite down on my bottom lip and squeeze my legs together as my finger vigorously taunts my clit. It gets more intense as I pull the lips and poke my pussy, and Done yanks and strokes his dick. Done's tongue glides across his dry lips as words escape in Espanola easing out and into my ears. Shit, that shit turns me on even more that I can't resist and invite him in to feel my wetness. He climbs on top of me and strokes me so passionately that we both shudder with excitement. That's one thing about Done he doesn't mind trying something different, especially if he's going to get a buzz out of it. And neither do I. Great wet sex is the best sex.

My cell phones rings.

I cut my eyes to the side wondering who could it be. The only person I can think of is Whupp. I roll over on the wet sheets and grab my phone out of my jacket pocket. "Hello."

"Hi, honey. I'm on my way home. You want me to pick you up some butter pecan ice cream?"

I smile. "Sure, honey."

"Baby, I'll be home shortly. I hope you're in the mood." He says.

"Huh?" I blink completely baffled.

"You know. We haven't been close in nearly two years. I think it is time to get back on the bandwagon. Be naked when I get home.

Love you."

"L-Love you, too." I cut my eyes at the phone. Then, I jump up and hurry and get dressed, peck Done on the forehead, and rush da hell home.

By the time I get there the house is still dark which let's me know Whupp hasn't arrived as of yet. I rush into our bathroom and fill the hot tub, burn some scented candles, run downstairs for a bottle of bubbly and ice bucket and bring it upstairs, find the right music, and soak my body in the warm soothing water waiting for Whupp to bring his old ass home.

Whupp comes strolling in humming: 15 Minutes: MARIO. I cut my eyes wondering what da hell has gotten into him. Then I sniff. *Damn, he smells good as hell*, I think to myself. And again, I cut my eyes a bit flustered. And to put the cherry on top of the sundae, Whupp kneels down and tongues me down. My head spins justa little. *Okay, what gives*, I think to myself? But then as we are swapping spit I really don't give a shit. Two years. Two! My man is finally back and I or rather *we* are going to fuck the night away.

2 hours later …

That man! If I have to kiss and tell all I can say is that Whupp fucked me like a gentleman. Every crack, crease, hole, did not go unnoticed. Whupp covered all bases and I in return covered him in juice, after juice, after juice—eleven times. I rained on him. I rained so much I thought I was going to dehydrate. Oh, that man!

I know you want the explicit details so here it goes.

Whupp gripped his dick—all 4½ inches (it shrunk over the years) of dark meat. He walked over to the hot tub; he spread his feet apart and stuck his dick in my mouth. Yep. Stuck. That shit turned me on! I loved when he showed aggression. I sucked his dick--balls and all. And Whupp loved every bit of *head* I delivered. Whupp got in the hot tub and I sucked his dick under water. Whupp moaned loudly and then said, "Oh, baby! Shit, baby, ba-by! Shit, shit, shit, ba-by!" Two years I wanted to suck that muthafucker raw. Whupp tried to resist the sensation but it was too good to resist. Whupp tilted his head back as his eyes squint. It was too much for him to take being out of the game for so long. Then, all of a sudden, Whupp flipped and grabbed my left tit. Then the right, and he squeezed them like he missed 'em. Oh, that shit turned me on even more. Then, he carried me to our king-sized bed. The same bed I fucked Done in. Whupp spread my wet legs and placed 'em both on his broad shoulders, stuck his dick in me and started stroking me with forceful thrusts. I mean hard thrusts. He stroked me so hard that he knocked a hole in the bedroom wall. Yes, he was fucking me hard and strong. And I loved every bit of it. He was a different Whupp. Each thrust grew more intense than the last. Oh, that maaaannnnnnnnnnn!

"Who's your muthafucking, husband?!" His eyes pierced mine and spit was spewing out of his mouth.

Whupp caught me totally off guard with this. But I didn't feed into it. Nope.

"You *Barracuda Bytch*, who's your muthafucking husband?!"

Okay, now I must admit I was little curious as to what he knew after calling me a *Barracuda Bytch*. I mean why else would he be asking me this question (*who's your muthafucking husband.*) What he's been sitting in that recliner so long that he forgot that he's my muthafucking husband? I didn't budge. Hell, no! Look, if I was caught I might as well have played this little drama episode out to the end.

But I will say Whupp didn't seem like he was playing because he practically had my head buried in the pillow. Now, I knew this muthafucker was not trying to suffocate my ass. But honestly, I couldn't be too sure. His body was hovering over mine, almost smothering me to death. Oh, shit I couldn't fuckin' breathe. His thrusts were getting harder and harder that I could literally feel Whupp's dick in my stomach. Oh, my... I thought to myself. What could I do at that point? Dive in and role-play: "whose your muthafucking husband." That's what da fuck I do.

Whupp grabbed me by my neck real hard and pumped his dick harder and harder so hard that my head bangs into the headboard. My eyes rolled in the back of my head. I felt this sensation building inside of me. Oh, shit I was about to EXPLODE! My toes eased into a stimulating curl. I started to feel fireworks, cherry bombs inside of me. Oh, shit, Oh, shit! I feel it! I really, really, fuckin' feel it! And then all of a sudden, Whupp's *dick* went limp. LIMP! LIMP, did you not hear me!

Okay, now I became the crackhead! Blacking da fuck out.

My mouth got to run 100 miles per minute. Head justa swayed from side to side. Neck snapped. My eyes bulged with disbelief. And pussy, oh, my pussy was swoll. Not, swollen. SWOLL. Pissed da fuck off!

OH SHIT!

OH, NO, MUTHAFUCKER!

I CAN'T BELIEVE THIS BULLSHIT!

All of those thoughts ran through my head. And Whupp just plopped on my sweaty titties, breathing like he was about to die and shit. All I wanted to say was please get the fuck off of me you two-year shriveled up dick no fucking ass loser. "Now, what the fuck are you going to do to keep my pussy happy?" Whupp looked dumbfounded. He didn't respond. Now I would've thought that Whupp would have used all of his "manly-tools" to make me cum. Not! That's what pissed me off even more. The man did not have a creative imagination. No toys up his sleeve. No backup plan. Nothing. Whupp had nothing. And I had nothing left to give either. So I got up, took a shower, got dressed and took my ass to see the one who would at least fuck me good. Yes, Done.

Whupp had better step-up his game or this pussy was on her way out for real.

LIMP "D"

I pace, pace, pace, stop, look down at D, and shake my head. Whupp, how did this happen, I ask myself. I sigh; suck my teeth, sigh, and stop. "I can't believe this shit, D! D, you were supposed to be my road dawg. What the fuck happened?!" I grip *him* in my right hand and try to choke his useless ass. "D, you let a brotha' down, man. Now, what the hell am I 'sposed to do about this…shit!"

I pace the floor swinging my shriveled up dick against my hot thigh. I look down at his shriveled up ass. "Look, D, Twat is a hell of a woman. Any man would feel blessed to have her in their life. This is my wife, man! I was depending on you to get me through this. I was depending on you to win my baby girl back and you let me down." I throw my arms up in the air. Man, I can't believe this shit!

"You gotta make this up to me, D. I don't know how but you better think of something and quick because my woman just left this house steaming mad. Her pussy is hot and bothered. And you know that is not a good sign." I look down at him. I wipe the sweat beads off of my forehead. "There ain't no telling where she might have ran off to. D, you better hope and pray that she doesn't find another *dick* to finish off what *you* tried to start. You sorry ass muthafucker!" I shake my head from side to side. "D, you better pray or we are going to have a problem. You hear me! We are going to have a real big problem."

I pick up my cell and call Twat.

Ring, ring, ring...

Ah, man, now she is not picking up.

C'mon, Twat, I say to myself.

I lower my head feeling just like dick.

I need to get out for some fresh air so I get dressed and head out. On my way to get in my car, my cell phone rings and it is my buddy Rufus.

"Hello."

"Yo man, what you wanna get into?"

"I dunno."

"Whoa, why you sound all down and shyt?"

"I dunno."

"I got the perfect remedy for that. Meet me over on Foreplay Drive over by TD Bank, park by the bank and wait for me, okay."

"What's over there?"

"You'll see."

"Aiight."

We hang up and I drive over to Foreplay Drive.

Rufus arrives and I hop in his corvette. He drives to this strip club Lipstick On My Collarbone and we grab a seat. The layout of the place is simple. The entrance is nothing but open space, a jukebox to the left, condom machine, and snack machine. The dance floor is in the middle with the sliding poles and all. The lighting is flashy; you know red, hot pink, anything that would set the mood of naughty, but nice. There is an open bar to the right with a barmaid who is fine, fine, fine. She is dressed in a skimpy tuxedo top letting her titties overflow with boy shorts showing off all of her ivory ass. But I like her boobs 'cause they are the size of gigantic melons. That baby is hot as hell! But the feast comes strutting on-stage with Prince panting in the background. This chick oozes sex. I mean oozes. From the tip of her blonde hair to her oversized titties, small waist, and that soft ass that is begging to be kissed makes dick rise to the occasion. *Down, boy, down.* Oh, she is sweet. Sweet. She immediately has dick perky. And I know if she comes any closer I am going to burst in my pants. My hand keeps slipping down to my thigh, and then eases over to dick and I want to massage that boy. Ooh, I want to grab him and stroke him vigorously. Damn, just watching this chick slide up and down that pole with her legs spread open is turning dick on. And when she twirls her sexy body around and around and then sticks out that long pierce tongue all I can think about is her sucking dick. That is the last straw. I lean over and whisper in Rufus's ear.

"Yo, man, I want her (Synthetic) to give me a lap dance."

"No problem, man."

Rufus throws up his right hand and signals the blonde bombshell to c'mere. Man, this chick is gorgeous as hell. D is eager to get his freak on. I feel him jumping in my pants. *Okay boy, hold on, hold da fuck on.*

Synthetic comes sashaying over to me and stands directly in front of me. *My, my, my, she is fine. Sexy. Damn.* Synthetic escorts me in this private room. D is standing at attention and I don't care who sees it. I sit in this mystery room and Synthetic does her thing. She touches me, all in my crotch area. She grabs dick and to my surprise she unzips him and teases him with small pecks. And I don't stop her. I know I've crossed the line but I am doing this to save my marriage. And then all of a sudden, dick is taken to this other world. Damn, it is slimy, and hot, and frickin' heaven to me. Synthetic suctions dick so skillfully she almost knock the wind out of a brother. I mean, I've had *head* before but not like this. The finale is when she makes me *come* in her mouth. My body trembles for mercy. I moan loudly expressing my appreciation for this blonde chick waking up dick. Of course, you know I broke her off real good. Walk out of the mystery room and tell Rufus let's head out. I am eager to get home and make love to my beautiful wife.

Rufus drops me off and I sit in my car and call Twat.

"Hey, hon, you home?"

"Yes."

"Go take a hot shower. Don't towel dry. Just lay on the bed wet and naked. I'm on my way."

"O-okayyyyy."

I get home and wifey is lying wet and naked on the bed with a chocolate covered bitten cherry inserted in her pussy lips. Man, that bitten cherry is drooling its sweet filling down her clit and I lean over and in as I scoop it up with my long hungry tongue. Damn, this woman turns me on. I can feel dick jumping. I am thrilled. I guess meeting Synthetic helped out a lot. I pull my dick out and climb on top of Twat and call myself stroking her good. I'm sweating like a pig but Twat ain't moaning or nothing. In my head I think I am hitting those right spots but in actuality I ain't hitting shit. Why? My brother D went limp, again. So you know what a brother does. I hurry and get myself up outta there before Twat flips. But I am not quick enough. As I am grabbing my boxers and pants all I hear is Twat mouthing off of how sorry of a muthafucker I am in bed. I rush to the bedroom door, down the stairs, and out the front door hoping Twat doesn't come outside making a mad-black-woman-scene. As I shut the door I hear a loud crash against the door. Brother wipes his forehead 'cause that was close. All I can do at this point is sleep in my car parked in our driveway and have another talk with D.

"Man, you set me up, D. I thought you were my boy. How come you were aroused with Synthetic but you can't do the same for *our* wife? Now, what the fuck am I gonna do? Don't even bother to answer that question 'cause you fucked up big time and Twat ain't tryna hear nothing from me or *you*."

I gaze at the sky realizing I need to talk to someone. I feel like I'm on the verge of losing her—the woman I have adored for years. My wife. My friend. Where do I go from here, I ask myself. And I swear I hear a little voice say to the chapel. Nah. I shake my head to that thinking that God might think I'ma damn fool for airing out my dirty laundry in His house. He may think I brought this on myself. He won't understand my infidelity. He may look at it as being my fault. That I contributed to my marriage failing. When all along I was trying to make my marriage work. Nah. I ain't going there.

I start my car and find myself driving to the nearest church I can find. It is as if I have no control over the steering wheel or something. I can't really explain it. Anyway, I step out and take a deep, deep breath. I walk up the six steps and wrap my sweaty hand around the doors handle and step inside. That's right. I step inside a place that is pure and quiet. I sit down in the open pew and let my soul speak with blunt honesty.

"Father God." I sigh.

I bow my head in shame.

"Lord, I have been unfaithful to my loving wife. I went with Rufus to this strip club called *Lipstick on my Collarbone*, and, and, this chick, excuse me, this woman named Synthetic pleasured a brother down. Well, I figured since I had problems with making love to my wife, and with Synthetic stimulating dick, I mean, my penis, I figured that "Ole' Whupp" was back and ready to please his woman. But Lord, it didn't happen that way. Nah. She is quite disgusted with me right about now. I don't know if I am impotent or what. Why is it that Dick, excuse me, my penis, won't get aroused enough to bust a nut inside my wife, Twat? I mean, she is beautiful, sexy as hell; I mean heck, any man would be honored to have her. And I do, but at the rate that I am going I question if I will be able to keep her.

"What more can I do? What am I doing wrong? Lord, can you talk to me? Here I am pouring my heart and soul out to You. Do you think I really want to confess my sins to you?"

I wait hoping for the Lord to speak to me, but it seems He has failed me too.

I storm out of the church mad as holy hell. I get in my car and just stare back at myself. Man, you really fucked up this time. You messed up big time, dude, so bad that God won't even talk to your doggish ass. Where can I go from here? The only person I can think of is Rufus. So I drive over to his house. Well, to my utter surprise Rufus is kinda cum-occupied with (you've guessed it) Synthetic. I ain't mad, dawg. Do you. That's right. Have your *happy ending*. I chuckle to myself and hop back in Ole' Girl (my car).

***

I sit at the kitchenette contemplating my death. Why? You may ask, because life has taken its toll on me. I am a man who has been blessed with every ailment known to man. You name it I got it. I'm doomed. The only thing that hasn't happened to me is that I don't get periods, but I do experience occasional mood swings. I can be a bit emotional, at times especially while watching Lifetime. What guy you know watches *Lifetime*. Me. I'ma broke down nigga. I used to be a manly man. I think I am getting in touch with my feminine side, at the very age of sixty-something. I know my age but do I have to broadcast it to the world. Look, I'm broken cut a man when he is down. I haven't crossed over to becoming a gay man, yet, but the thought has crossed my mind...once. And it had my head spinning. My palms open as my face lands smack dab in the middle of my smooth as butter hands. I never had to do hard labor. I was most fortunate, but now. I dunno how women handle being women.

I was one of those lucky guys. You know, the kind of guy who got the right job. The right woman. The right house. The right car. Timing was always right for me. I was the kind of guy who excelled in pretty much everything his heart desired. The kind of guy that wanted for nothing yet yearned for everything and got it. That was I... Whupp D. Twat. I was *that* man. That was who I used to be, but life changed all of that.

The lucky guy I used to be had come face-to-face with hardships and heartache. I, after twenty-nineteen years had been fired from my job as an architectural engineer. Then my wife Twat after many wonderful years decided she needed a change of scenery, which was I. She packed her bags and left me for a woman. That was a hard blow. I had no inclining that she was so unhappy. I mean I gave her the world. But I guess the world I gave wasn't big enough to fill the void of me working like a slave. She often said she missed me. I was trying to give her the moon and stars. And in the midst of me trying to woo her, someone else wooed her.

One-day things seemed good and the next things went bad. It hit me hard that she left, but it really kicked my manhood's ass that she left me for an ugly woman. Lord, that was an ugly girl. I dunno what Twat saw in her. It had to be that inner beauty that Oprah was always talking about 'cause that girl was a hideous sight to be seen. Man, oh man, I stayed locked up in my bedroom over that for nearly a month. It was that devastating to my ego. I loved that woman more than she'd ever know. Sometimes I wished I could hate her. Yeah, just sometimes I'd wished but deep down I love her too much to hate her. I know. I got it bad. Tell me something I don't know. She is my soft spot. What I wouldn't do to have her back with me. She says she's happy. How happy, I wonder.

After losing my job, and later retiring, and after losing my woman, too, I received some disturbing news that the man I never considered to be my father had died from carbon monoxide poisoning. It was the wee hours when I received the phone call from an old buddy of mine. The word "died" nearly blinded me. But to make matters worse what nearly took me out for real was when I found out that *he* didn't have any life insurance or a burial plot. The entire burden was left in my hands because I was their only child. I just assumed they had their house in order, but as it is said assuming makes one an ass. I was the ultimate ass.

Sometime after that it seemed I took ill rather quickly. If I started out with one thing I'd end with another. Burdens were heavy. And that led to me drinking, smoking, gambling, and dealing with loose women who ain't amount to much but an easy lay. I wasn't looking for love. I was looking for something to fill the void of emptiness. I searched and searched and searched but I was unsuccessful in finding it. Yet, my primary doctor kept finding more and more and more things wrong with me. I was always a man of good health. But like I said life took its toll. And love wore me down. Quite frankly, I am tired. So very tired that I walked into Droppin'-Like-Flies

Funeral Home and started the prearrangements upon my death. I already had a mausoleum and plot. I have no children so there is no need to do a living will or will. I decide to let my wife fight the battle of getting anything that I own after I am dead. This is my gift to her for leaving me. I have no fight left in me to quarrel. I am simply undone and beaten to a pulp that any life left is merely a waste. I was ready to go. Cut my loses. Throw in the towel and meet my savior. Yes, I am ready to die.

One way or another it is bound to happen. I just want to be prepared if and when that beam of light comes shining through. I keep my house clean. I put it up for sale, but no one has bid on it. I emptied out my bank accounts. Any 401k's I have. I ended my partnership with my buddy, Rufus at our soul food restaurant in *The Dawgs House* in Newark, New Jersey. Any pension that was due to me I have submitted in my paperwork to start receiving it early. I took the penalty for early withdrawal, what the hell. I even decided to write a book about my life, but it seemed like a waste of time because I have nothing good to share. All it will do is collect dust and I don't need any more failures in my life. One seems too many and two seems to push me over the edge. I am a shattered man.

***

"Whupp's beat down"

Since I am ready to die I decide to make myself easy prey. I decide to take a stroll over to my cousin's house that lives on the east side of town, but instead I make a detour. There I stand in the heart of the "ghetto" bling down from my neck to my wrists. It is broad daylight on 110th Street in the 'hood of Arson. Yeah. I lean against my spanking new Bentley with an Armani suit on and some alligator shoes with a knot of hundreds in my hand, waiting on the crowded street of no-mans-land. I am waiting for that desperate soul to come and take me out.

I am pumped for the first blow to knock the shit outta me. Stomp me down until I bled to death. Shove a ten-inch knife in my flesh and slice me like sushi. I wait and wait and wait and no one approaches me. I even turn the car radio up loud to attract attention to myself. Heads turn but they stand still. *Something is wrong with this picture,*

111

I think to myself. *With all of these thugs in the mix why hasn't anyone snuck up on me?* I throw my arms up in the air. *Can a brotha get jumped? What is the deal!*

By 1:00 a.m. I give up. Shove my money in my pockets. I hop in my car to head home and as I am about to exit out of the parking space these thugs in a white van block my way. Six men in masks jump out and yank me out of the car. I smile. It is the best feeling in the world. One punches me in the face and I immediately feel my eye swell the size of a boiled egg. Then another guy hits me in the back of the head with what feels like a bat. I cackle loudly. Then another guy kicks me in my groin so hard I feel it tickle in my throat. I slump over and the pain is electric. I want more. Another guy hands roams through my pockets and snatches out three thousand dollars. I grin from ear to ear. I just know that they are going to end my day with a loud bang. Another guy pulls out a gun and I want to kiss that baby hello. And the last guy snatches the gun away from his friend and my eyes squint as a wrinkle spreads across my forehead. I am livid. *What the hell*, I think. *I am ready to die. Let my man do it*, I think, again. I sulk with such disgust so I provoke the situation to make all of them mad.

I start shouting, "HELP, HELP, HELP!"

It angers one of the guys to the point that he snatches me by the collar of my designer shirt and knocks me to the ground pointing the gun to my head. I am chanting, yeah, yeah, yeah with enthusiasm. Break a bone. Crack my skull. Puncture a lung. Do something, please? The rush with death is thrilling. I am eager to feel the pain of that hot, burning sensation poke a hole in my head. POW, POW, POW...I am ready.

DO IT!

I keep repeating these words in my mind.

DO IT!

I look him dead in his eyes, waiting. I start humming, "*Help a brotha out.*" I am so anxious for him to take me out of my misery.

DO IT!

But somehow the trigger gets stuck. *This is some bullshit*, I think. I cut my eyes to the side and try to signal him to use my man's gun and shoot that sucker. Yes, I am quite aware that I am referring to myself.

These are amateurs, I think. Where are the "real" thugs?

To put a damper on my moment of glory I hear sirens and the thugs rush off leaving my Bentley. And the guy who emptied out my pockets gives me back my three grand. What the hell?! You gotta be kidding me, I say to myself.

Can a black man get shot, puuuullllllllleeeaasssssseeeeee?

***

"Whupp setting himself ablaze"

I am brainstorming in my bedroom. I get some good sleep, but I am most disappointed that I didn't die in my sleep. God must be preoccupied so I still have to take matters into my own hands. What can a brotha' do to die? I ponder over this question. Then it hits me as I stare at a green lighter on my nightstand.

I leap out of bed and take a long hot shower. I get dressed in some beat-up jeans, a wife-beater T, and some country looking sandals and I walk into the owners garage and nosey around for a red container for gasoline. I find one. Then I hop in my Bentley and head for Chucks Gasoline Station ten miles away from my home.

Once arriving at the gas station I greet Chuck, himself.

"Hey, how you been?"

"Well, well, well, looka here. Look what the cat drags in." Chuck says, with a sly grin on his dark-skinned face.

I reach in the backseat and grab the red container to fill it with gasoline. I am so eager to get back home that I pay the clerk and zoom off into the sea of fresh dew morning air.

Once I arrive back home I leave my car parked outside of the garage. I enter my home and I place the gasoline on the floor near the living room entrance. I start pacing trying to build my nerve up. This is gonna be big. I mean this is going to be bigger than I'd imagine once the damage is done. I pick up the phone and call my wife and leave a brief message: "REMEMBER WHEN YOU TOLD ME TO DROP DEAD, Twat? WELL, YOU ARE FINALLY GONNA GET YOUR WISH. I HOPE YOU'RE HAPPY!" I hang up with a huge smile on my face. I stand in place for a moment or two thinking of whom to call next and then it hits me, my ex-boss. So I pick up the phone.

"Hello, THE ISLEY GROUP, How may I direct your call?" a soft-spoken woman's voice asks.

"Ma'am is Mr. Harry Webster still employed there?"

"Yes. Who may I ask is calling?"

"This is Whupp D. Twat, ma'am."

"Just one moment, sir, I'll transfer you through."

"Thank you, ma'am."

"Mr. Webster speaking."

My eyes light up.

"Mr. Webster, this is Whupp D. Twat. I don't know if you remember me, sir, but I was a dedicated employee to your firm for many, many years. I just called to express my thoughts of you." With a straightness of face I say, "You sir, are an IDIOT! You know nothing about architecture or people. You are clueless. I don't know the moron who gave you the title for which you hold. It had to be nepotism! You are a waste of living being. Just breathing up all the air. Why don't you croak and make my life happier!"

I can hear his hard breathing in the phone like his temples are about to burst any minute. I am hoping that they do. I hated him as a boss. I hang up feeling rejuvenated. This is the boost I need to die.

I walk over and grab the red container of gasoline. Then I pace the floor with the container in my hand trying to decide which room should I die in. The bedroom. The kitchenette. The dining room. The fully furnished basement. The bathroom. Or where I am standing which is the living room. Okay, the living room it is, I say to myself. I take a long glimpse at myself in the mirror above the mantle. I look shabby. Five o'clock shadow, bags underneath my eyes. Fat face. And my hair that looks like silver spray paint all over my head. I am *old* and homely looking. I nod my head in agreement. It is time. So I douse the living room floor, first. I grab my favorite recliner chair and sit in it as I douse my sandals, pants, and wife-beater T. I pat my pockets down for a match. Nothing. I stand out of the chair and check throughout the house for a book of matches. Nothing. The gasoline smell is making me lightheaded. Yet, I am determined to find me some matches so that I can set myself ablaze. I rush through each room in the house and still nothing. I know that I can't call a neighbor over. He or she will blow the whistle on me and I won't be able to die. Then, it hits me the green lighter on the nightstand. I rush upstairs only to find that the lighter that was once full is now empty. I scratch my scalp on that. I'm the only one here so how can it be empty, I wonder. Then another idea races through my head—the stove.

I rush in the kitchenette and turn the knob to the stove and nothing. No flames, nothing. I tighten my lips hot, burning mad. I am ready to die, Lord!

I tap my forehead flustered. I can't call the repair guy to come fix my stove so that I can die right after. This is most disappointing. I even get daring trying to rub a stick and a rock together—a stick and stick together—a rock and rock together hoping to spark a flame. I even think about tampering with the outlets. Nothing works.

I grow tired. I undress and take a cold shower because I am already burning hot. *This is some bull-crap*, I think to myself. I should be burning right about now. I should be up in flames glued to the recliner chair. The house should be ablaze by now.

I drop my head so full of dismay.

Why can't I die?

The next day, I hear a thump on my front porch. I walk to the door and open it only to find a newspaper. I have no subscription for the local newspaper. *Maybe the newspaper boy made a mistake and delivered it to the wrong house.* I shrug my shoulders and pick up the newspaper and shut the door. I am brewing a pot of coffee. My stove is still broke. I am about to pick up the phone to call the repairman when I hear a thump at my door. So I put the phone back in its cradle and walk to the door and open it. All I see is a newspaper so I pick it up and close the door.

I sit at the kitchenette table skimming through the paper until I reach the obituary section and there it is plain as day. My eyes spread big staring at a picture of Mr. Webster. At this moment I feel powerful. *If you speak it it shall be done*, I think. So I start speaking it about myself. Every chance I can get I ask God to let me die. And every day I seem to live to see another grueling day. What is wrong with this picture, I ask myself scratching my scalp. I don't know. Only God can answer this and at the moment He isn't returning my calls.

***

"Whupp wrestling w/a Pit-bull"

I am strolling pass my neighbor, Mr. Frederick's home when he stops me to say hello. He is patting a dog, a rather ferocious dog.

"That's your dog, Mr. Frederick?" I ask, standing a few feet away.

115

Mr. Frederick looks up with those sea-blue eyes. "Yes. This is my baby, Killer."

"KILLER?" I say, with smirk on my face.

"Yes Killer. This dog is a fighter dog. The meanest I've seen." He says, massaging the dog's ears.

"Oh yeah. How so?" I am quite intrigued.

"Oh, Killer will rip you to shreds. Tear into your limbs like paper. I put hot sauce in each meal. Right, Killer." Mr. Frederick grips its face. "That's a good girl."

"Girl!" I shriek.

"Yes, Killer is a girl. She had enough of dogs doing her dirty so I trained her to be a hateful bitch."

"You don't say." I say, pondering with a glow in my eyes.

"Oh yes, if she doesn't know you and you come close to her she is liable to kill you."

I chuckle, as Mr. Frederick cut his eyes at my private humor.

"Well, Mr. Frederick, I best be heading home."

"Well, don't be a stranger."

"Good day."

Immediately, I feel devilish on my way home. Demented thoughts are running fast through my head. Death is the new high in my life. I am destined to die.

I open my front door and sniff. It smells too clean in here. But with these grisly thoughts I am having it makes me famish for a juicy chuck steak. I figured I'd eat well so that I taste the same as Killer devours me. Chuck steak, it will be!

I wash my hands, open the MayTag refrigerator and pull out the Chuck steak. I remove it from its packaging, season it with sea salt and pepper and garnish it with fresh garlic and parsley, and drench it with Worcestershire sauce. I pull out two Idaho potatoes and rinse them off and place them in the oven to bake, but then I realize I hadn't called the repairman to come and fix the stove. Okay, so I decide to pull out my grill, but then I realize I have no lighter fluid, charcoal, or matches so I have no choice but to pull some aluminum foil from its packaging and wrap it and set it in the refrigerator to marinade. That leaves me with no choice but to drive over to Nadine's Diner for a bite to eat.

I arrive at Nadine's Diner and eat a hamburger and French fries and gulp down a Pepsi, and leave.

On my way home, I stop at the nearest store to pick up some matches, lighter fluid, and charcoal. My mind starts racing back to setting myself ablaze, but the sweet taste has dissipated from my tongue. I want to move on to bigger and better things. Killer—that ferocious white and brown spotted bitch with those long fangs for teeth. A chill runs through my spine just thinking about her eating me alive. I actually get a hard-on from her image. So I think I might as well pleasure myself for the last time. What the heck! Soon I'd be a slab of mutilated meat placed in a black body bag. Dare to dream.

Once stepping foot in my home, I get undress down in the living room. Down to my birthday suit. I sit in my recliner and close my eyes and yank on Ole' Billy Bo. I call him that because he used to be smooth with the ladies, back in the day. The women loved themselves some Ole' Billy Bo. They loved the way he stroked them. He was the "man" like no other.

I decide to treat myself to a hooker because I want to feel the softness of a woman. Smell her pussy and taste her residue on my tongue. So I get dress, grab my keys, and head out to find some stank dirty pussy. It doesn't take long for me to spot her. Long legs. She has those full and soft juicy lips. And them chocolaty eyes of hers that seduce me. Curvaceous body. Mocha skin. She reminds me of my wife (well, not quite because Twat's pussy was always sweet and tasty.) My eyes droop at her. I want her. So I pull up along side of her and ask her to hop in my ride. And she does, after I flash some cash in her face. As we are riding along I ask her. "What's your name?" And she replies, "Holliday, baby." I smirk 'cause I figure this trick must be something special to be calling herself Holliday. I hope we have a merry time. Instead of taking her to a cheap motel I take her home and bang her all night long. She sucks Ole' Billy Bo and I am on fuckin' cloud nine. It is the best feeling in the world hearing her scream some other jokers' name. That bitch screams and screams. So I play along, "Scream bitch, scream!" Then I hear her scream out: Dick, Done, Rufus (my dawg), Kake, Twat! Fuck, I don't care. Shit, I don't even care about myself. *Whoa!!!! Did she just scream Twat?!!!* I cut my eyes to the side while she is on her knees sucking my dick.

Wait a minute, did she say *Twat*, I say to myself. Oh, that shit pisses me off so I slap that bitch. Then I twist her slender ass around and fuck her in it. Fuck protection, I say to myself. BITCH, KILL ME! KILL A BROTHER!!! I just know after sexing a dirty whore she will inflict me with a deadly disease. I just know it. But this whore is different. She shows me a fuckin' record of all of her annual visits to the doctor. You gotta be fuckin' kidding me, I say to myself. I never knew a whore could be so damn clean. But this one is. Brother can't even contract an STI or STD or whatever it's called.

Shit. Where are the whores with Herpes? Gonorrhea? Something? Brother can't even contract HIV/AIDS. What da fuck! I thought this was America. This is supposed to be the land of the free. Well, dammit, I am tired of being free, single, broke, and womanless. I want my Twat. My muthafucking Twat!

***

"Whupp on YouTube"

I get back in my broke down Oldsmobile feeling like shit. I head to the bar on Broom Ave and get my drink on. As I am sitting there I sip on my gin and juice and glance at the TV. Before I am incoherent I see this chick on "YouTube" justa shaking her ass and popping that pussy. *Bingo!*

Okay, I think of the perfect way to profess my love to Twat. Yep. Go on www.youtube.com and broadcast my undying love for her as I explain my dilemma to the world. I love Twat. This is the *only* reason I am putting myself to shame in front of a million people. Because without her I ain't shit. I need help and God won't talk to a brother so I feel I have no other alternative but to resort to these measures.

The next day…

I sleep in my car waiting for Twat to leave our home. Man, she looks good as hell. After she drives off I stroll in the house as if we are the happiest couple on the block to the outside world. I speak to my neighbor, Mr. Jones, and walk in the house.

Okay, get naked, I say to myself. As I am walking up *our* stairs I pull off every layer of clothing making a trail to our study where the computer resides. I turn on the computer and get myself ready to shoot my video of me in my most vulnerable state of being and mind. There I am butt naked in front of the camera airing out the fact that I have a limp dick to the world. I plead for someone, anyone to hit me up and suggest something to arouse me and keep me hard enough to fuck my wife's brains out. I know that this is embarrassing to the male population but I love my woman. I will jump over hoops for this woman. Professing my love for her is the only way I see of getting her back. If this doesn't work I guess I'll jump in the Great Falls and die an already shattered man. I sigh, again.

I upload my video called "LIMP DICK" and let the world see what I have to work with. Yes, this shriveled up lil' fellah who is making my life a living hell.

TWAT

I'm pissed! Truthfully, I am going through a lot of shit. You see I left Whupp and here I am dealing with an ugly woman who fulfills my needs but I dread taking her ugly ass out in public. I know, I can't have my cake and eat it too, but that is all about to change. Twat is about to bounce. Okay, you already know my routine. When shit gets tough I call Done. I was not going to let him go. It has been about a month, but I don't care. If Done claims to love the pussy he'll embrace me with open arms. I can't do this carpet licking shit much longer. Hell no! *I need some dick!*

Until Whupp gets it through his thick head that I am a woman of substance. I have needs that have not been met for two years and I have patiently been waiting for him to crawl out of his dark hole and fuck me right. That day almost presented itself but Whupp went limp on a sister. What am I supposed to do? Wait. No. I've done that for two years and I have nothing to keep me happy. Whupp stopped taking me out in public. He stopped taking showers with me. He stopped being affectionate to me. He stopped rubbing my back and feet. He stopped looking at me butt naked or cuddling with me in bed. He stopped making me feel beautiful. He stopped appreciating the little I had to give him, which he said was the reason he fell in love with me in the first place. He stopped, not me. Him! So what am I supposed to do, stop living because he is going through something? No. Twat is living for Twat. I have to please myself in every way possible. But it doesn't hurt to have someone willing to please me. No, it doesn't. So that is why I am going back to find that one who is willing to try. Yes, Done.

Here I was giving all I had to try to make my marriage work and all I got was kibbles and bits like some fuckin' puppy. Whupp stopped caring about me. And I stopped caring to care.

In spite of everything I get a call from Song Byrd that Whupp is on YouTube with his shriveled up dick. I burst out laughing, at first. But then I get angry at the world seeing my man's shit. I chuckle again. Fuck it, I say to myself. Finally he has gotten some balls to do something foolish. That is a turn on for me.

A few days later I call Whupp and we talk. About a week and a half later I decide to give our marriage another chance. I figured what do I have to lose. Hell, I've lost him once.

Oh, if you're wondering Whupp's video on YouTube received 100,000 hits within seconds time. Yeah. It seems those bitches loved my Whupp—limp dick and all. After the beat down, Whupp got his shit together and he has been stroking my twat strong. I kicked Synthetic to the curb. Not bad for a sixty-something year old chick, huh? Yeah, not muthafucking bad, wouldn't you say?

Oh, just to let you know I enrolled in an Anger Management Class. Whupp and I are in marriage counseling to save what is left of our marriage. We are also seeing a Sex Therapist too. Not for me. I have no problems when it comes to fucking. See, I ain't as bad as yous thought. I love my Whupp. And Whupp loves his Twat.

Look! That's the story and I am sticking to it!

IT IS!

IT IS!

IT IS!

Tears burst from my eyes. I tilt my head back and squint my eyes pleading to forget. I don't wanna remember. God, please? Why do I have to go there? Why?

Yes, I love Whupp.

BUT

I know it is not fair to me.

BUT

I know that he is having a difficult time.

BUT

I know he's …

BUT

I know…

BUT

But I don't want …

DONE/TWAT

"Baby, I'm heading out to shoot some pool with Rufus."

"Alright." I say, while in the kitchen washing a sink full of dirty dishes. I was cooking up a storm for Whupp. Yep. Trying to salvage what was left of our marriage. At least I was trying.

As soon as Whupp walks out the door the phone rings. It's about 9:03 p.m. I towel dry my hands and answer the phone.

"Hello?"

"Wassup, Twat?"

"Done?"

"Yeah. Were you busy? What's been going on?"

"Same ol' same ol'. Taking it easy, you know."

"Hmmm. Well, you feel like coming out."

I pause.

"You there?"

"Uh-huh, I'm here. You know I'm in this Anger Management Program."

Now, why did I tell him that?

"No. I didn't know that."

"Yeah, well, I'm still working on my marriage."

"Look, I understand that, but won't you just come out for a bit. Let us catch up. I'm in school and I have a test tomorrow. Maybe you can help me study."

"That's great! What are you taking up in school? But Done you don't need *me* to help you study."

"Yeah, I do. Air conditioning and refrigeration is my trade."

"You and I both know that we will not get much work done because anytime we are around one another you know what happens."

"Nah. You can help me study. I won't touch you."

I had to pull the receiver from my ear and stare at it for a second. "Ah."

"If you like I'll come pick you up."

My eyes cut to the side. "You'll pick me up? Do you have a car?"

"I got my boys ride."

"Oh."

"Aiight?"

"O-kay." I cave.

We hang up and I go into the bedroom and grab my favorite holey jeans (in the knees) and a T-shirt with my stiletto green boots and a jacket, keys, and my lucky green hat. About twenty minutes later the phone rings.

"Hello."

"I'm outside up the street from your house."

"Okay. I'm walking out the door now."

As I am about to walk out the door, I grab a piece of paper and leave Whupp a note saying that I am staying by Lollipop's house because she is having some man issues with Shadow—her worthless ass dope fiend boyfriend.

Once I arrive at this blue Mustang, Done gets out and opens the door for me. *He is such a gentleman.*

"Hi."

"Wassup, baby? You look and smell great!"

"Don't get no ideas, Done." I say, checking his fine ass out.

God, help me with this one, please? I am sitting next to this fine ass man and my body is yearning to be tied up and gagged. What is a girl to do?

"You aiight?" Done ask, while turning the corner on Brewer Street.

I nod my head up and down.

"You sure, Twat. You are too quiet."

I turn in his direction and look into those eyes and say, "Baby, I am fine."

"That you are."

I smile.

After a while of talking my body calms down. Done parks across the street from his house and then he says, "You want a beer?"

"No."

"Just a beer ain't gonna do nothing to you."

"Didn't you say you have to study?"

He stands and makes this funny face as if to say Twat c'mon.

I finally give in and we head to the corner liquor store. Done get's a Colt 45, Natural Ice for me, and some pork skins, and then we head to his house.

He turns the TV on. I take off my jacket as he reaches for it to hang it over the chair. I am always comfortable at Done's house so I take off my boots and wiggle my pretty toes. Done sits down and tunes into basketball game. I lean back as he opens my beer. I take a sip. A few minutes later, Done pulls out some papers and starts writing some stuff down. I grab one sheet and start quizzing him to see how much he has absorbed.

"Okay, you ready? Tell me if this is True or False."

"Shoot."

"That's right, Done."

I keep asking random questions just to throw him off a bit. About fifteen minutes into quizzing him I realize Done needs to study a little more so that he can get an A on this test. By 12:00 a.m. Done puts his test down and leans back and yawns. I am already snuggled in the bed with nothing on but my tie-dye panties and a nightshirt that says LOVE. Done climbs in bed and I snuggle under his hot-blooded skin. His hands massage my arm, and then it slowly massages my thigh, and glides up to my left breast.

"Done, no, go to sleep."

He stops, but then tries again.

"Done, no, you said that you wanted me to help you study. You said that you could lie next to me without touching me. You're such a liar."

Done stops touching me and we lay still. But then, his hands have a mind of their own and he starts trying to unfasten my bra, but he can't figure out how to unfasten it. Then his hands slither downward and massage my twat.

"No, Done go to sleep so that you won't be late for school in the morning."

"You really want me to stop?"

"Yes."

"You sure?"

"Yes, you are so spoiled."

"You spoiled me."

"I know. Now I'm going to un-spoil you."

Immediately, Done stops. But then, this rush of heat swelters my body. A part of me wants Done to touch me, but he doesn't and I don't initiate anything. But what I do is unfasten my bra and fling it over on the chair. I just lay there hoping that he'll try one last time. And within a few minutes he does. His hot hand glides up and under my nightshirt and squeezes my breasts like an orange. He pulls on my nipples and that excites me even more. My eyes close and I let out a moan wanting more. Then his hands glide down to my twat and I can feel my juices flowing, heavy, like it is about to pour with wetness. Goodness, it feeeeellllls so fuckin' good!!! We are both laying on our side and Done spreads my ass and insert his hard dick in my twat. I am slippery wet, so wet that you can hear the wetness as he humps me inward and outward. I grab the pillow and squeeze because it feels so good to my body. I don't want him to stop. The room is heating up and I am on fire.

"Turn over?"

I do just that. Spread my legs and let Done feed me from behind. Not doggy-style but from behind and I squeeze the pillow again taking it all in. Taking him, all of him in. Done turns me over on my back, spread my legs, open me up, and eat me out.

My eyes flutter as I feel his long tongue masturbating my clit.

"There?"

"There?"

"There?"

"There?"

"*Ohhhhhhhhhhhhhhhhhhhhhhhhhhhhhhhhhhhhhhhhhhhhhhhhhhhhhh hhhhhhhhhhhhhhhhhhhhhhhhhhhhhhhhhhhhhhhhhhhhhhhhhhhhhhh hhhhhhhhhhhhhhhhhhhhhhhhhhhhhhhhhhhhhhhhhhhhhhhhhhhhhhh hhhhhhhhhhhhhhhhhhhhhhhhhhhhhhhhhhhhhhhhhhhhhhhhhhhhhhh hhhhhhhhhhhhhhhhhhhhhhhhhhhhhhhhhhhhhhhhhhhhhhhhhhhhhhh hhhhhhhhhhhhhhhhhhhhhhhhhhhhhhhhhhhhhhhhhhhhhhhhhhhhhh*…Yes, there." I moan and bat my lashes.

I don't know what is going on with Done but he loves me so good that I want to cry. Not rain but actually cry…crocodile tears. Me. He raises my legs above his shoulder blades and licks my pussy and teases my clit with the tip of his hot tongue. My arms reach out to grab something but there is nothing but air. Honestly, I have never felt like this before. I don't know what to do with myself. I start pulling my nipples, squeezing my titties trying to fight the feeling. I start rubbing his baldhead. I started tugging on my hair. Damn near pulling it from the roots. My whole body is under his command. Done is taking me on a ride I have never been on before and I don't know how to react. In other words Done is putting the "Puerto-Rican Whammy" on me. That has *never* happened to me before. Never.

His tongue twists; curls, and does some trick that make my body shudder like I am about to have a seizure. His hot finger pokes deep into my wet hole. My arms spread like angle wings and my toes curl as I feel it. Oh, Oh, Oh, Oh!!!!! I feel it about to burst inside and out of me.

"Oh, Donnneeeeee! Oh, ba-b-yyyyyyy! Oh, you bilingual-dick! Oh, oh, oh, oh!" That's all I can say as I feel it building so intensely that I want to crawl the fuckin' walls like that cockroach I see crawling up his bedroom wall.

His slimy tongue drives me insane and all I can do at this point is cum. I cum so hard that I want to scream but no sound will come out. That "Puerto-Rican Whammy" had my ass speechless. For once, I had experienced a baptism from one man making me cry without me doing any of the work. And I must say having this extra umbrella *cums* in handy. So what is a girl to do now?

Listen, experiencing that "Puerto-Rican Whammy" has open me up to something new. And of course, I want more. I can see that this is going to create a problem as far as my marriage is concerned. But how often does this happen to a woman of my stature?

Done put it on me and there is no looking back. I am a fiend. Addicted to his multi-talented tongue. It is the best of both worlds because Done loves for me to rain. And I love for Done to make my twat cry…crocodile tears.

As far as Whupp is concerned that limp dick isn't going anywhere. Not because I say so, but because his love is that strong for me. And mine is for him. It isn't about sex with us. It is about love. I love Whupp with heart and soul, but I have to keep that extra umbrella because I still want to feel desired and Done keeps me alive. Without him…well my pussy will probably dry the fuck up and die. And once that dies, I die. And as you know, I am too young to be thinking about death. My twat is happy. And so is my heart. I have the best of both worlds. And yes, things could most certainly go wrong, but I am keeping an open mind that this is meant to be. Done makes me cry while he was fucking da shit outta me. He broke the code. The muthafucker broke the fuckin' PUSSY code. I can't believe this shit! *I* finally cried.

TWAT

I messed up big-time. I didn't know until after. Um, um… Kommon and Whupp are related. Yep. They're half brothers. I didn't know until Whupp and I started dating. And till this day Whupp has not let me live it down that I gave my baby, his nephew up for adoption. Why? Because we have no children of our own. That's why. If I had met Whupp instead of Kommon— knowing the man that *he* is I probably would've kept my baby, but that wasn't the case. I lower my head. It wasn't.

Around this time was when my attitude changed. I changed. And there was no looking back. Chocolate Twat was here to stay. But the sensitive part of me cried.

I cried for the big lil' girl in me. I cried because my mama never accepted me. I cried because I was hurting after my daddy died. I cried for my baby. I cried because Whupp wouldn't make love to me for two years. I cried because I was afraid of aging and feeling like my youthfulness was fading away from me.

In that moment I cried for Chocolate Tease. I cried for her because she suffered in her thick skin for many, many years until I became the woman I am now…Chocolate Twat. And I'd be damn if I ever look back. I love my thickness. Every thick piece is more than a mouthful for my man and my extra umbrella—Done. That's right!

Listen, every woman has her preference. Not all have sexcapades. Some are faithful to their mates. But me, I have to have my extra umbrella because I never know when I may feel the urge to rain. The feel of liquid pouring down is so exhilarating. So liberating that you will feel on top of your game knowing that your man has *never* experienced such a cum shower before. And if he doesn't enjoy it, honey, you may want to check the sugar jar to see how many cubes are missing, oooookkkkkkkkkkkkkkkk. Don't suck your teeth at me I'm trying to help you sister-girl.

Look, that's on you 'cause my twat is always super duper wet. Don't black da fuck out, cry, whine like a lil' bitch, or lose yourself over a man. Puuuleeeaaaassssseee, Sister-Girlllllllllllllll, get a grip on a new dick. With the assortment of umbrellas out in this world, girl, go and get you another umbrella and call it a…not Valentine's Day, Christmas Day, or Thanksgiving Day. You know what you do. Call it a Fucking Day and get your groove ooooooonnnnnnnn!

DONE/TWAT

BLACK DA FUCK OUT!

Done's cell phone rings.

"Why won't you answer your phone?" I ask.

"'Cause I don't feel like it."

I feel my hormones racing. "I can't do *this* anymore, Done."

He just looks at me. "What happened between last night and this morning, huh?"

"Everything." I say with conviction.

He lay back on the bed unconcerned.

I cut my eyes at him. "You're enjoying this, aren't you? You like having *her* there and *me* here, don't you? Answer me?!"

Silence.

I stand up. "Look at me and tell me that you don't enjoy having your Kake and eating me too."

Silence.

Done eyes pierce mine. "If I wasn't in this relationship with *her* we wouldn't be having this conversation."

I pierce his dreamy eyes. "That is not true because she is never here. She doesn't exist to me because she is never seen. That's not the reason for this conversation." I pace the floor.

"We made love last night. We ate. Watched TV. And made love, again."

"Yes, I know I was there remember. I must have stuck on stupid plastered across my forehead."

His eyes continue to pierce mine. "I take that as an insult."

I snap back to the bitch I can be. "You can take it any way you want because I really don't care, anymore."

"Look, Twat, I don't want you leaving my home angry. Let's talk calmly about this."

I roll my eyes and purse my lips. "There is nothing left to say unless you admit that you are enjoying this. This doesn't bother you one bit, does it? You like the attention. You like her calling with me laying next to you."

He stares into my eyes and smirks.

That just pisses me off. "ANSWER ME?! YOU LIKE THIS DON'T YOU?! THIS DOESN'T BOTHER YOU, DOES IT?!"

"No. It doesn't bother me, Twat. But I told you about her. I like you Twat. I like you because you don't beat around the bush with your words. You say what's on your mind. I like the way you make me feel. I like feeling you next to me. We fit, baby."

"Yes, I know you told me a lot of things to get what you wanted. You are no different than the rest of the assholes I've dealt with."

That hit a nerve in him. He raised his head and cut his eyes at me. "You're comparing me to the men who hurt you. I'm not them. I'm different. You never had a man like me, and you know it."

I wave my hand. "Oh, please, Done. You're just like them with your charm. You lure women in your web and use that debonair bullshit to have your way with them. You do things that they haven't had in a while just to seem sincere, but you're not. You're just like them."

Done stands up and meets me face-to-face. "I'm different in spite of what you might think. What's really going on with you, Twat? You actin' *realll* strange, you know. What's with the mood swings, emotional roller coaster bullshit? You act like you pregnant or something."

My mouth spreads wide open and I slowly sit down on the edge of the bed. "Pregnant, don't be silly. Get da fuck outta here wit' dat dumb shit." I smirked. "I'm too young to be pregnant." *Pregnant? Menopause? Pregnant? Nah?*

Done just stares at me, "Yeah, you're too old to be pregnant with *my* baby." Oh, that was a cheap shot after he'd fuck me then he insults me. Ain't that some shit!

I don't want to hear shit about being old and pregnant. Nah. That is not true. And I have to prove it to myself.

URBANE FLAVOR

"Damn! He is tall and sexy," I say to myself. Mmmmmmm. I am on the prowl for something new and exciting and there this Adonis stands waiting to be snatched up. This is the scene we have played as if we don't know each other but we know one another very well.

He is a long not-too-long-ago fuck. The kind of fuck that left my pussy swoll. And I don't mean pissed off, either. He'd fuck me so good that my shit would be hurtin' fo' days. That man gotta dick on him that was like a lethal weapon. I kid you not. And he is fine. Damnnnnnnnnnnn! That is a fine ass man!

We have electricity. Fire. The attraction between us is unheard of. He makes my body singe. My twat is sloppy wet. And I keep his dick hard as a rock. His balls are the size of two peaches. Oh, and they taste yum-yum. His demeanor is smooth. Debonair, yet he has swagger. He speaks Ebonics but I don't give a fuck. He can fuck! That's all that matters to me after that comment Done had said about me being *old*. Fuck him!

It is Sunday in August. The humidity is treacherous to my skin and hair. Shit I am glistening where niggas keep asking me if am I knocked up. Fuck y'all, I say to myself.

I think of Urbane Flavor. I press his digits on my cellular.

"Hello."

"What's good, Twat?"

"You baby."

I always get straight to the point with him. I am already moist from hearing his voice. Yeah, brotha have that kinda potent shit that makes my pussy squirt through the muthafuckin' phone.

"When you want to see me?" Urbane asks all sexy and shit.

"When can you be seen wit' your fine self?"

We love to play the "Chase Game", but we make sure we get caught.

"Oh, you tryna gas a nigga's head up and shit."

"Nah. I only speak the truth."

"Where you at?" he asks.

I reply. "Where you always know where to find me."

"I'll be pulling up in a few minutes."

I hop on his bus and Urbane drives his patrons to the Meadowlands. As soon as everyone departs off the bus, Urbane takes me by the hand and leads me to the back of the bus. He only has a 15-minute break before picking up his patrons. He yanks my green thong down and dives his humongous dick right in my shit. He cracks my ass open and sticks his dick so far that my eyes cross. I am on all fours and taking it like a champ. I open my legs wider and let his "Boy" talk to me. We have that kinda kinky shit going on. No games. He loves the freak in me and I adore the street in him. We are like dynamite together. His 6-foot height, cashew-colored skin and big 9½ dick is like Christmas to me. I am on top even though I am taking it from the back. He is doin' me strong. Pouncing my ass. Shit, I am taking head and all until he hits the bottom of my pit and spits his cream all in my shit.

Shhhhhiiiiiiiiittttttttttttttttttttttttttttttttttttttttttttttttt! I am young and full of cum. Nah, I don't cum because I don't want my panties soaking wet. Urbane hands me a baby wipe and I wipe coochie clean, pull up my panties, and sit my ass back down in the front seat as if nothing happened. That shit was spontaneous. Just what a twat like me needed. I needed to be pumped and Urbane did me right. I realize that I don't always have to be in the driver's seat. Sometimes a chick likes dat ass to be cracked. Yeah sometimes.

Well, Done ditched Kake. We stopped fucking and now I only have dealings with Urbane. Look I ain't no fool. I know any day Whupp's dick could go limp again. A sista needs to be fed regardless if I'm married or not. Dick and Kake got together and now his tired ass knocked her da fuck up. My girl Synthetic, oh, she got knocked off for messing wit' somebody's man. And no, it wasn't me. I wouldn't kill da bitch. Look, her dumb ass got caught in the chick's bed. Ain't nobody tell her to get high wit' him. She was just supposed to suck his dick and move the fuck on. She moved the fuck on aiight. R.I.P Synthetic.

Looks like everybody got whom he or she wanted; I guess the question remains if they are able to keep 'em.

WHUPP "D"!

"9-1-1. Dispatch. Sergeant Littleton. What's your emergency?" 14:00 HOURS.

"Listen to me clearly. My name is Whupp D. Twat. I live on 277 Liverpool Ave—the big ass yellow house (but you already know that because I'm calling from home) I got my wife butt naked kneeling on her knees wit' a sawed-off shotgun pointed in her mouth. Now, she only got one choice either suck my dick wit' you on the phone or die."

"Whupp D, you say your name is? Lemme…lemme talk to your wife?"

"Yeah, that's my name. Nah. Cain't do that." 14:01 HOURS.

"Listen, it can't be that serious. Why don't you try talking about it before you do something you will regret."

"WHAT! Talk! Look, ain't nobody playin' here. I will blow her fuckin' brains out!"

"Why would you want to do that to your beautiful wife?" 14:02 HOURS.

I scrunch up my nose. "BEAUTIFUL! Beautiful! This Barracuda Bytch ain't beautiful. Triflin' ass hoe. She'a hoe. A broke down hoe." I snatch the plastic bag off the loveseat and pull out an orange wig. "Bitch, put this on your head." So she does. Then, I grab this colorful bag from *Free People* that she had her new halter-top in and I make her use it as a dress. "Put this on, now!" and she does. "Keep those shoes on," I say. I pull the full-length mirror out from the corner of the room and lean it against the wall. I reach for my camera. "Look in the mirror, bitch! Admire yourself. You *love* you more than you *love* me," I sneer, as I place the phone down and snap, snap, snap.

"Talk to me Whupp? Tell me what happened? Whupp? Whupp? Whupp? Where are you, man? Talk to me?" Sergeant Littleton says in assertive tone.

14:03 HOURS.

I pick up the phone and finish my conversation. "Nah. I'm tired of talking and reasoning and being a punk-ass nigga. All I want *her* to do is suck my dick wit' you on the phone. She out here trickin' an' shit fo' these broke down nigga's out here while I'm tryin' to fix my *shit*. I'm tryna get "D" back to where he usedta be. Ok. So I'm suffering from erectile dysfunction. But I give her everything a woman could ask fo' and she gonna disrespect me like this. She can't be there for me during this difficult time. Nah. She out here fucking: Done (I grew up wit' him). Then there was Dick (a former co-worker of mine). And then she had the nerve to fuck Urbane (that's my first cousin). Nah. Nah. If she can fuck those jokers and suck their dicks she can suck my shit, too! I'M HER HUSBAND!!!!!"

14:04 HOURS.

"Listen, Whupp, I learned a long time ago from my father to never leave my woman in the company of family or friends. No disrespect but you set yourself up. Somewhere you let your problem down below get in the way of your marriage. Ask her. Ask her if she missed you. Ask her if she needed you. You probably disregarded her feelings because of your own hang-ups. She got tired and lonely. I know that she's a beautiful woman still trying to keep her youthfulness. She's trying to stay sexy and vibrant for you. And you know it too. You don't need me on the phone man. You need to communicate with your wife."

"Nah. Nah. We are beyond communicating. She crossed the line! We'll communicate when I shove my dick in her mouth. She had too many chances already and she kept fucking. She just wouldn't stop. Nah. I want this recorded so stay on the line or else."

"Okay. Don't do anything to escalate this, Whupp. I get it. You're trying to make a statement of some sort. Lemme talk to her, man."

"Yeah. I want you to hear how good she gives *head*. I told you she cain't come to the phone!"

14:06 HOURS.

"Calm down, Whupp. I didn't mean to get you upset. What's your wife's name?"

"Why you wanna know? You plan on fucking her too?"
14:08 HOURS.

"Nah man. Just curious that's all."

"Yeah, I bet."

"Seriously. I got my own bitch at home and she get on my fuckin' nerves too."
14:10 HOURS.

"Uh-huh."

"It's true. I asked her to suck my cock the other night and she ignored me."
14:11 HOURS.

"Man, stop playin'."

"No. It's true."

"So what you do? I woulda beat her ass and shoved my dick in her mouth and told her to shut the fuck up! I handle mine."

"No. I let it slide."
14:12 HOURS.

"You punk-ass nigga. I woulda beat that bitch ass. Straight up."
Silence.

"Why you so quiet, Whupp?"

"'Cause I got dis bitch stroking my shit."

"She's sucking your cock?"
14:14 HOURS.

"Nah. She's jerking it off, but I'm 'bout to shove my dick in her mouth 'cause she playin' wit' my emotions."

"How so? I mean you got a gun pointed in her mouth so how can she be playin'?"

"She's slick. The bitch is slick. Out here fuckin' around on *me*! (eyes spread wide) I'm the nice guy. Well, I usedta be. She had it good. And then she fucked it up! You don't know her like I do. (forehead sweating profusely) I understand why now."

"What do you mean, *now*, Whupp?"

"Growing up my dad Big Whupp left when I was nine. He met another woman and started having an affair on my mom Bump. It hit me hard. Big Whupp was the opposite of me. I never wanted to be like him. I wanted to be a good guy, but I realize good guys get shitted on. These bitches out here don't want a good guy, nah. They want a muthafucker to beat their stuck-up asses. To slap and punch 'em around. Tattooing their bodies with black and blue marks that they consider to be love taps. The shit is twisted. Sick! I get it. Twat never wanted a good guy. Nah. She considers me to be her *bitch—her* punk-ass nigga all because I respected her and treated her like a queen. I loved her! And she took me for granted (nodding my head up and down) how that song goes, Twat?"

"I,I,I d-u-n-no." she says with lips trembling and her voice cracking scared out of her mind.

"Oh, slut you know. Um, "If Tonight Is My Last" by that chick um, um, Laura…Laura Izibor. Yo just listen."

I start singing the song in acappella.

"Whupp, lemme talk to her?" Sergeant Littleton asks.

I stop singing. "Nah. I cain't, serge."

"Well, lemme ask you a question."

"Shoot."

"How did you find out about the other *men*? I mean not to toot your wife's horn but she covered her tracks pretty well."

I lean my head back and chuckle like a psychopath killer. Then I stare at Twat burning a hole in her head. "I had my informant." I smirk, as Twat kneels on her knees with her ass mid-air.

Rat-a-tat-tat!

"Bohemia POLICE! OPEN UP!!!!!!"

14:17 HOURS.

POP! POP! POP!

CONFESSION

Now you know the truth. Well, actually, you don't. See Song Byrd got in contact with the prison to do an interview with me. Um, she had already interviewed Twat a while ago. That girl knew how to talk. Boy did she. So I decided to talk, to tell my side of the story. I tried to be a good decent man to Twat. I tried. But brotha' snapped and now I am doing *life* for killing my wife. I killed her by *crackin' dat ass* with the power of a sawed-off shotgun. BOOM! (Closing my eyes) blood…her blood splattered everywhere. It was grisly. Every time I close my eyes I see *her*. I experience nightmares of me pulling that trigger. I don't know what happened, but I became someone I never thought I could become. *I* became a *murderer*. I lost it. Completely lost it. The rage was so intense. The pain was so severe. I wanted her to hurt like I hurt. And she did. Believe you me. She did. It was a done deal. Twat didn't stand a chance of surviving. She died in our living room. Yeah, it's fucked up. I fucked up.

I took a leap of faith when I decided to combine our stories into a book. Ironically, Karla, the founder of *The Write Message*, contacted me through a letter when she read the article written by Song Byrd in the November issue of *What Ticks* wanting to bring *our* story to life. I guess you're wondering why I decided to tell my story to the world.

Well, for one she was willing to listen. I felt I could do it. I mean I knew Twat like the back of my hand. Well, at least I thought I did. I know everyone has a story to tell but how many will confess some shit like this. Most men wouldn't want to admit such an act but I'm trying to break the cycle. I'm trying to be a better man. I owe it to Twat. It would be a slap in the face if I didn't feel any remorse. Now, that would be fucked up. Nah. I couldn't punk out like that. Twat was my world. And in a half of a second's time I changed all of that. I did it! Me. The *good* guy. The good guy snapped.

Now I am in *Mid State Correctional Facility* in Wrightstown, New Jersey. I felt it was important to share. It was a way of healing for me. Forgiving myself for the sinful act of taking a human's life. My wife. Of course, I wish I could turn back the hands of time. I miss her. You don't have to believe me. Twat meant everything to me. Oh, I loved that woman to death (lowering my head with tears flowing down my face.) She will always be my Chocolate Twat. I'll never forget her. I wanted something of her. Yes, I have memories of her, but I needed something else. I decided a tattoo of Twat would be nice. Being in prison that was gonna be hard to do, but where there is a want, there is a way. I never wanted to forget her. Never. I know that my life will never be the same. I don't need anyone to tell me that. I already know. I'm getting much older. And life for me takes on a whole new meaning. I'll never be free in the physical sense, but I'm learning to be free in the mental and spiritual sense.

Anyway, one day during recreation I spoke to my boy named Spike. I told him that I wanted a tattoo. Spike hooked me up with a tattoo on my back. It took about a week to complete it, but Spike did his thing. Yeah. I want to sleep with her every night until I take my last breath. Yeah. That's my twat—my Chocolate Twat. I lower my head as tears run down my face. *Baby, I'm sorry. I'm sooo sorry.*

R.I.P
BARRACUDA BYTCH
1944-2009

Acknowledgments

I gotta give a shout out to my boy, FRANKIE FLOWERS for putting a dainty sister like myself on to some good shit as we were in deep conversation at Grill 77 (on Washington Street downtown Paterson) getting our breakfast on. I mean all Frankie said was the word: barracuda. And the next thing you know within a half a second I came up with the title: *Barracuda Bytch*, but I didn't share that information with Frankie. Then my mind started racing and the end result is this book in your hands. Yep. It was just that damn simple. I was on it for sho'. If any of you don't know I'm not the type of writer/author that waits around…time waits for no one. I take heed to that. Thanks for the talk, Frankie.

To my boy "JENTLEMAN THUG" a.k.a DeWitt, I gotta say with all sincerity I appreciate you trusting me with some need-to-know information allowing me to make this book what it is. On the real, I couldn't have done it without you. Brotha' keep on writing 'cause there might be a part two to this shit. Good lookin' out. You charming muthafucker!!!!

To my photographer, DON SHERRILL, man, you've done it again!!!! Every time I find myself breaking out of that shy shell. And you know what it feels dammmmmmmmnnnnnn good. Thanks for being so professional.

Currently she is working on her next book:
I Cried B'tween My Legs- Lust, Love, and Life Lessons
(a memoir)
She resides in Paterson, New Jersey.